ROWAN had never disappointed the bukshah. He had never let *them* down. In the frosty early mornings or in the heat of the sun, when they were injured, or giving birth to their calves, or when they needed comfort as the Dragon roared, he had been there.

Now they needed water. They would not expect him to fail them. To them he was not an undersized, scared weakling. To them he was leader, guide, and friend. They trusted him absolutely. The thought flowed through him like warm, rich milk.

He raised his head and looked straight at Strong John. "I will go," he said. The map he held fluttered in the little breeze that always came before the dawn. "I will go with you to the Mountain."

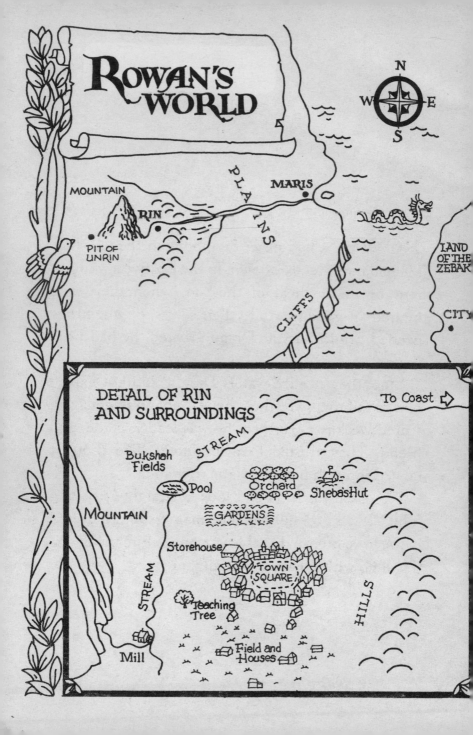

EMILY RODDA
ROWAN
of RIN

A Greenwillow Book

■ HarperTrophy®
An Imprint of HarperCollinsPublishers

Rowan of Rin
Copyright © 1993 by Emily Rodda

First published in Australia in 1993 by Omnibus Books,
an imprint of Scholastic Australia Pty Ltd.
First published in the United States in 2001 by Greenwillow Books,
an imprint of HarperCollins Publishers, by arrangement
with Scholastic Australia Pty Ltd.

The text of this book is set in Weiss.

Map copyright © 2001 by Lynn Sweat

Library of Congress Cataloging-in-Publication Data

Rodda, Emily.
Rowan of Rin / Emily Rodda.
p.   cm.
"Greenwillow Books."
Sequel: Rowan and the Travelers.
Summary: Because only he can read the magical map, young, weak, and timid Rowan
joins six other villagers to climb a mountain and try to restore their water supply, as
fears of a dragon and other horrors threaten to drive them back.
ISBN 0-06-029707-7 (trade) — ISBN 0-06-029708-5 (lib. bdg.)
ISBN 0-06-441019-6 (pbk.)
[1. Heroes—Fiction.   2. Fantasy.]   I. Title.
PZ7.R5996 Ro 2001   [Fic]—dc21   00-063619

For Alex and Clem

CONTENTS

1 ∾ THE MEETING

One morning the people of Rin woke to find that the stream that flowed down the Mountain and through their village had slowed to a trickle. By nightfall even that small flow had stopped. The mill wheel lay idle. There was no water to turn its heavy blades. The bukshah drinking pool on the other side of the village was still. No bubbling stream was stirring it into life and keeping it topped up to the brim.

There was no change on the second day, or the third. By the fourth day the water in the pool was thick and brown. The bukshah shook their heavy heads and pawed the ground when they went to drink in the morning and the evening.

After five days the pool was so shallow that even little Annad, who was only five years old, could touch the bottom with her hand without getting her sleeve wet. And still the stream failed to flow.

On the evening of the sixth day the worried people met in the market square to talk. "The bukshah could not drink at all today," said Lann, the oldest person in the village and once the greatest fighter. "If we do not act soon, they will die."

"Not Star," whispered Annad to her brother, who was the keeper of the bukshah. "Star will not die, though, will she, Rowan? Because you will give Star water from our well."

"Bukshah cannot drink from our well, Annad," said Rowan. "It is not sweet enough for them. It makes them ill. They can only drink the water that flows down from the Mountain. It has always been so. If the stream stays dry, Star will die like all the rest."

Annad began to sob quietly. The children of Rin were not supposed to cry, but Annad was very young, and she loved Star. Rowan stared straight ahead. His eyes were tearless, but his chest and throat ached with sadness and fear. The sadness was for Star, his friend and the strongest and gentlest of all the bukshah. And for all the other great, humped woolly beasts, each of which he knew by name. But the fear was for himself. For himself and Annad and their mother and indeed for the whole village.

Rowan knew, as Annad did not, that without the bukshah there would be no rich, creamy milk to drink, no cheese, curd, and butter to eat. There would be no thick gray wool for cloth. There would be no help to plow the fields or carry in the harvest. There would be no broad backs to bear the burdens on the long journeys down to the coast to trade with the clever, silent Maris folk. The life of Rin depended on the bukshah. Without them, the village, too, would die.

Annad could not imagine the valley without the village. But Rowan could. Reading the old stories in the house of books, listening half asleep to Timon under the teaching tree, and, most of all, sitting on the grass by the stream while the bukshah grazed around him in the silence of the morning, he had often imagined this place as the first settlers must have seen it.

Hundreds of years ago they had climbed through the hills, carrying the few things they owned on their backs, looking for somewhere in this strange land that they could claim as their own. They had come from far away, across the sea. They had fought a terrible enemy. On the coast they had heard, from the wandering native people they called the Travelers, of a place at the bottom of a forbidden mountain in the high country far inland. They had been tramping for many, many days in search of it. They were very tired. Some had almost given up hope. Then, one afternoon, they had topped a rise and looked down. There below them, nestled between a towering mountain ahead and the hill on which they stood, was a green, secret valley.

The people stared, speechless. They saw trees loaded with small blue fruits and fields of flowers they did not recognize. They saw a stream, and a pool, and a herd of strange gray beasts lifting their heads to stare, horns shining in the sun. They saw silence, stillness, and rich earth, and peace. The people knew then that this was the place. This would be their home. So they came down and mingled with the big, gentle animals, who were tame and unafraid. They called them the bukshah.

"The stream flows down from the Mountain," said Bronden the furniture maker, her loud voice breaking into Rowan's thoughts. He watched her stab the air with her stubby finger, pointing. "So the problem must be up there. Up there, something is amiss. Something is stopping the flow."

All eyes turned to the Mountain rising high above the village, its tip shrouded as always in cloud.

"We must climb the Mountain and find out what it is," Bronden went on. "This is our only chance."

"No!" Neel the potter shook his head. "We cannot climb the Mountain. Even the Travelers do not venture there. Terrible dangers await anyone who dares. And at the top—the Dragon."

Bronden sneered at him. "You are talking like a crazy Traveler yourself, Neel! There is no Dragon. The Dragon is a story told to children to make them behave. If there was a Dragon, we would have seen it. It would prey on the bukshah—and on us."

"Perhaps it takes its prey elsewhere. We do not know, Bronden." Allun the baker's light, pleasant voice rose above the muttering of the crowd. "But if you will excuse me for talking like a crazy Traveler— remembering that my father was one, and it is only to be expected—let me remind you of what we do know." His usually smiling face was grim as he stared Bronden down. "We do know that we hear it roar almost every morning and every night. And that we see its fire in the cloud."

Bronden rolled her eyes disdainfully, but Rowan shivered. Tending the bukshah in the cold and dark of winter mornings and in the evenings when the sun had slipped behind the Mountain, he had heard the sound of the Dragon. He had seen its fire, too, in the sky above the cloud. The bukshah swayed and grew restless at these times. The calves bellowed, and the bigger beasts pawed the ground, flared their nostrils, and huddled together in fear. Even Star moaned when the Dragon roared, and when he stroked her neck to calm her, he would feel the nerves jumping under her long, soft wool.

Suddenly he realized something no one else seemed to have thought of. He must speak. Nervously he rose to his feet. The villagers stared curiously at him. What could the boy Rowan, the shy, timid herder of the bukshah, have to say?

"The Dragon has not roared since the stream dried up," said Rowan. "Not in the mornings, and not at night." He spoke as loudly as he could, but his voice sounded small in the silence. He sank back to his place.

"Is this so?" Allun looked around the circle. "Is the boy mistaken?"

"No, he is not," said Bronden slowly. "I recall it now. Indeed, there has been no sound from the Mountain for days." She lifted her head. "So I am right. There is something amiss, high above us. I have told you what we must do."

"But we cannot do it," insisted Neel with dread. "The Mountain is too steep, too dangerous. We cannot climb it."

"Has anyone ever tried?" inquired Allun.

"Yes!" said tall, straight-backed Marlie, the weaver and dyer of cloth. "In times gone by some people *did* climb the Mountain, to look for new fruits to plant in our orchard. But they never returned. After that, the people of Rin heeded the warning and left the Mountain alone."

"You see?" Neel burst out. "You see? If we climb the Mountain, we will die."

"But, Neel," boomed Bronden. "If we do *not* climb the Mountain, we will die."

"Bronden is right. We must make our choice," said Strong Jonn, who was the keeper of the orchard. "We remain here and hope the stream begins running again of its own accord, or we climb the Mountain and try to remove whatever is stopping the water from flowing down to us. Both ways are dangerous. What is our decision? To go, or to stay?"

"We must go," Marlie replied. "We cannot simply stand by and let death slowly come to our village. I vote to go."

"And I," shouted Bronden.

"I vote yes!" said Strong Jonn.

"I, too," added Allun lightly.

"Yes! We agree!" growled mighty Val the miller, who had stood silently listening in the shadows, shoulder to shoulder as always with Ellis, her twin brother. Val and Ellis toiled together in the mill, grinding the grain into flour, endlessly cleaning the great stone building so that not a speck of dirt or the tiniest spiderweb could be seen within its walls. Jiller, Rowan's mother, said that since childhood no one had ever seen them apart.

"Yes!" "Yes!" "Yes!" One by one the villagers stood up. Rowan looked around at the familiar faces, now so serious and so stern. Maise, the keeper of the books, was standing, with her son and daughter. So were Timon, the teacher, and Bree and Hanna from the gardens. White-haired Lann leaned on her stick beside them. And even fat, soft Solla, who made sweet toffees and cakes and never could resist his own cooking, had struggled to his feet. Then Rowan saw Jiller rise slowly and join them. His heart thudding with fear, he scrambled to his feet beside her.

Soon Neel the potter and four others were the only ones still seated.

"So it is decided," cried Bronden triumphantly. "We will arm ourselves and set out at dawn."

"Wait!" said Marlie. "We must not go without consulting Sheba."

"That mad old hag? That spinner of children's nightmares and curer of pains in the belly? What has she got to do with this?"

"Sheba is old, Bronden, but she is not mad," said

Marlie firmly. "As anyone who has been cured of illness by her remedies will tell you, Sheba knows more than herbs and spells. She understands the Mountain as you and I never will. Sheba knows the way up the Mountain. The secret way she was taught by the Wise Woman before her. We must ask Sheba to help us."

"This is a good idea," agreed Strong Jonn.

The people murmured. Many did not trust the Wise Woman, Sheba. She lived alone beyond the orchard, gathering herbs and other growing things and selling the medicines, ointments, and dyes she made from them. She rarely spoke to anyone other than those with whom she traded. And when she did, it was seldom pleasant. The children of Rin were a hardy crew, like all of their race. But they were afraid of Sheba and called her not Wise Woman but Witch.

"Oh, come! What harm can it do?" called Allun, grinning. "If the old one can tell us anything, which I doubt, then all the better. If she cannot, we have lost nothing."

"Travelers' foolishness!" snapped Bronden. "This is not a game, Allun the baker. Why don't you—"

"Enough!" cried old Lann. She glanced at Bronden, who scowled. "We are going into the unknown," she said sternly. "And time is precious. We cannot afford to miss a chance to speed our way. Who knows Sheba best?"

"I know her," said Strong Jonn. "She gathers an herb that grows under the hoopberry trees in the orchard."

"I trade with her," said Marlie. "Her purple and blue dyes, in return for cloth."

"Then you two can go and beg her favor," said Bronden, "since you are so keen to do so." She turned her back on them.

"We will wait here for your return," said Allun. "Be speedy. There is much to plan." He laughed. "And take care not to insult her, now. Like Bronden, she is not a woman to be trifled with."

Strong Jonn looked around at the watching villagers and pointed. Rowan jumped. Jonn's finger was pointing at him!

"Boy Rowan," called Strong Jonn. "Little rabbit, herder of the bukshah! Run and get two cheeses from the coolhouse. The oldest, ripest, strongest cheeses from the topmost shelf. And bring them to us at Sheba's hut. Sheba is very fond of good, strong cheese. The gift will sweeten her temper."

Rowan stared, openmouthed, and did not move. He was terrified of Sheba. His mother nudged him. "I will go," piped up little Annad, beside him. "I am not frightened." Laughter rippled through the crowd.

"Go along, Rowan," Jiller urged in a whisper. "Do as you are bid. At once!"

Rowan scuttled away through the crowd.

"He is scared of his shadow, that boy," he heard Val the miller mutter to her brother as he passed them. "He will never be the man his father was."

Ellis grunted agreement.

Rowan ran on, his cheeks burning with shame.

2 ⌒ SHEBA

Rowan was panting when he reached the coolhouse. Trembling, he climbed the ladder and took two of the oldest cheeses from their shelf. The coolhouse was packed with cheeses, vats of smooth white milk curd, churns of butter. Plenty for everyone. But not for long, if new supplies did not replace the old.

He left the coolhouse and hurried toward the orchard beyond which lay Sheba's hut. He could hear the sound of the crowd still assembled in the market square and was glad he didn't have to pass them on his way. As he reached the outskirts of the village, he thought about what Val had said. Stumbling slightly in the ragged grass, he began moving through the hoopberry trees, dodging the twisted, hanging branches. He thought about Sefton, his father.

Sefton had come home from the market late one night, just after Annad was born, to find his house burning. A log had rolled from the fire and set the ground floor on fire. Flames were licking the staircase, and the house was filled with smoke. Sefton had shouted for help, then leaped up the burning stairs. He had pulled the unconscious Jiller and the new baby from their beds and carried them down to safety. Then, as the flames burned higher and hotter, he threw a blanket around his head and went back into the house—for Rowan, in the attic. No one could stop him, they said later, though the heat and smoke beat everyone else back. Even the giant millers, Val and Ellis. Even Strong Jonn, Sefton's friend.

They saw Sefton at the attic window, with Rowan in his arms. They saw him fling the window open, and heard him cry out. They rushed to catch what he threw to them—his son, screaming in terror, wrapped tightly in the rug from his bed. And then they heard a crash and saw the roof fall in and the flames leap and roar. Strong Jonn, cradling Rowan in his huge arms, gave a shout of grief. Sefton had saved his family. But he had gone from them, forever.

Rowan grew up knowing that his father had died to save him. He knew, too, that although they never said so openly, many people in the village of Rin felt that the exchange had not been a fair one. The villagers were farmers and traders now, but they were descended from great warriors. And in their time, when Rin was threatened, many of the older ones had fought to defend it. The War of the Plains was alive in their memories and recorded in dozens of volumes in the house of books. The people of Rin were proud of their tradition of courage.

At an early age every village child learned to run, climb, jump, swim—and fight. Rowan had trained with the others, but he had never been good at anything. He had always been small for his age. He had always been shy. And since the night of the fire he had been even quieter and more nervous than before. Val was right, he thought. He would never be the man his father was. And neither would he have the strength of his mother, who since his father's death had worked even harder, plowing the wheat fields with Star, planting and gathering the crop, taking it to the mill.

Rowan had been given the job of herding the bukshah because it was easy. Tending the big, gentle beasts needed no strong arm or great courage.

Only once, years ago, had a keeper of the bukshah come to grief. And the mine shaft into which she had fallen trying to save a wandering calf had been closed in long ago. A much smaller child than Rowan could have done the work. But he was allowed to remain with his beasts, and for this he was grateful.

The bukshah loved him and knew his voice. They would look at him with their soft brown eyes and nuzzle his hand when he was sad, as if they knew his troubles. In return he tried to make their lives comfortable, learning to cure their ills, treating their cuts and bruises as his mother treated his, combing burrs and prickles from their woolly coats. When the winter snows blew in the valley, he would bring the old and weak to shelter, for he knew that the freezing winds could kill them, and he could not bear to lose even one. In the spring, when the blossom of the orchard sweetened the air, he would run and play with the calves and carry them handfuls of new peas he stole from the gardens when no one was looking.

Rowan listened. He could hear the beasts now in their field nearby, rumbling and snuffling to one another as the sun began to dip behind the Mountain. He wished he was with them, instead of tripping over his own feet in the orchard with his arms full of smelly cheeses and his head full of shameful fears.

He scrambled through the fence that marked the orchard boundary, and his steps slowed as he saw light flickering from Sheba's hut. Despite the coolness of the evening air, her door was open, and gigantic shadows wavered and crept on the strange, pale grass that grew before it. He began to tremble again as he approached.

Two of Bree and Hanna's children had once told him that Sheba could turn you into a fat slug if she chose. They pointed to the slugs that they were picking from the cabbage leaves. "These were all people, once," they said. "Look—that's our uncle Arthal there. We know him by the spot on his forehead. He gave the Witch a rotten tomato in a bag he traded for bellyache medicine. One rotten tomato in a bag of twenty. And that's what she did to him. Good-bye, Uncle Arthal. Hello, Uncle Slug. Want to give him a kiss?" They had pushed the writhing creature up to Rowan's mouth and hooted after him as he ran away.

Rowan knew they had been teasing him. He knew it, really. But sometimes in bed at night, or if a bukshah strayed and he had to go near Sheba's hut to catch it, the children's story would come back to him, and he would remember the slow, fat slug with the spot on its forehead, and shudder.

Voices drifted out to meet him as he trod softly among the shadows on the grass. Strong Jonn and Marlie. And another voice, cracked and low. Sheba.

"The stream flows down from the mountaintop, above the cloud," she was saying. "Under the earth and rock it flows, to Rin. And so you must climb the Mountain, to the very top, my fine friends. And none knows the secret way but Sheba!" Her mocking laugh rang out.

Rowan thought of putting the cheeses down on the doorstep and running home. But as he stepped forward, a twig snapped under the toe of his boot.

"At last!" Strong Jonn's head popped out the door. He put his arm behind Rowan's back and propelled him inside. "The boy with the cheeses. Our gift to you, Sheba," he said heartily. "In trade for your knowledge of the way."

The old woman sitting by the fire sniffed the air and smacked her lips with a greedy sound. "The cheeses!" she gloated. Then she frowned, and her eyes narrowed. "Bring them here," she ordered. "Closer, boy."

Rowan hesitated. Marlie, beside him, gave him a little push. His feet felt like stones. He forced them forward, a step at a time.

"What are you hiding?" snapped Sheba, half rising from her chair. "I said closer, boy! Come here and put these famous cheeses in my lap. For how do I know that I am not being cheated? Fobbed off with second-class goods?"

"They are the best we have, Sheba," said Marlie. "Rowan chose them himself, from the highest shelf in the coolhouse. You will like them."

"So you say." Sheba scowled as she hunched her shoulders and stared at Rowan. In the firelight her eyes looked red. Her forehead was bound with a purple rag, and her hair hung like thin gray tails around her face. She smelled of ash and dust, old cloth and bitter herbs. Rowan reached her chair, placed the round yellow cheeses on her lap, and backed swiftly away, holding his breath, trying not to look at her.

But Sheba had lost interest in him. She was prodding the cheeses with her bony fingers, sniffing them one by one. Rowan hugged himself and shuddered, sheltering behind the tall figure of Marlie from those terrible red eyes. What if he had chosen badly? What if the cheeses were no good after all? What if Sheba thought he was trying to trick her?

The old woman looked up. "They are good," she pronounced. "As good as you said they would be, Jonn of the Orchard."

"Naturally." Strong Jonn bowed to her.

"Now, Sheba," said Marlie firmly. "Will you tell us what we wish to know?"

"Ah, brave Marlie!" Sheba giggled unpleasantly. She took some sticks from a basket beside her and threw them on the fire. It flared up as the sticks caught alight, and shadows danced on her face as she turned back to them. "Brave as you weave your cloth safe at home and dream of glory. But how brave will you be on the Mountain? The Mountain has ways of taming big brave girls like Marlie, if they are so foolish as to try their strength against it. It has ways . . . so many ways . . . as you will discover."

Rowan felt Marlie stiffen and saw her cheek begin to burn red. "We do not need your warnings, Sheba," she said in a level voice.

"And Jonn! Strong Jonn, keeper of the trees! Fine, tall man!" jeered the old woman, ignoring her. "Now you come here to ask me favors. But what were you but a raggedy, bare-bottomed little boy like all the rest once upon a time, crying for your mama when Sheba passed by?" She bared her long brown teeth at him in a hideous grin. "The Mountain will not test your strength, Jonn. It will destroy it. As it has destroyed the strength of men with twice your courage. You will twist and blubber like a baby in the grip of the Mountain. But the Mountain will not let you go."

There was a moment's silence. Rowan was rigid with horror.

Strong Jonn laughed. Then he planted his hands on his hips and addressed the old woman sternly. "Quit your tales, Sheba!" he said. "They are wasted on me and Marlie. The boy Rowan is the only one to fear them here. You should not think us so foolish as to follow his example. Look, you have scared him half to death, poor skinny little rabbit. And he picked you such excellent cheeses, too! You should beg his pardon."

Sheba went on grinning, but her eyes shone scarlet. "Laugh, then, Jonn of the Orchard," she sneered. "If the boy is the only one afraid, he is the only one of you with sense. It would do you no harm to be guided by him!" She again reached down into the basket beside her. "And so indeed, I must beg his pardon," she cackled. Then, fast as a striking snake, she threw a stick straight at Marlie, who yelled and jumped aside in her fright, leaving Rowan to take the full blow of the flying wood.

Rowan stumbled back and nearly fell, the stick clutched in his hand and blood beginning to drip from a gash in his forehead. Strong Jonn exclaimed in anger and stepped forward with clenched fists.

"A gift from Sheba," snarled the old woman. "And I do beg your pardon, Rowan of the Bukshah."

"Sheba, you go too far!" thundered Strong Jonn.

Her lips curved. "Do I so?" she said. "Well then, perhaps this meeting should be ended."

"Not until you have told us what we came to hear," cried Marlie. She glanced at Rowan, cowering in the shadows. "And quickly! The boy's forehead must be attended to."

"It's only a scratch," said Sheba placidly. "But still, I grow weary. I am tired of your childishness. I will tell you what you need to know. As far as I am able. Wait."

She lay back in her chair and half closed her eyes. Her hands stroked the cheeses in her lap as though they were cats. The fire glowed. She began to drone and mumble to herself. For a long time they could make no sense of her words. And then at last she spoke clearly:

> "Seven hearts the journey make.
> Seven ways the hearts will break.
> Bravest heart will carry on
> When sleep is death, and hope is gone.
> Look in the fiery jaws of fear
> And see the answer white and clear,
> Then throw away all thoughts of home,
> For only then your quest is done."

Sheba's eyelids fluttered, and her eyes opened. For a moment she stared blankly at Jonn, Marlie, and Rowan, as though wondering why they were there, then her expression sharpened, and she waved her hand at them impatiently. She no longer looked like a witch. Just a tired, crabby old woman.

"Go now," she said. "I can tell you no more."

"But the way, Sheba. The way we must go," urged Marlie. "You have told us nothing!"

"Have I not? Well, we will see. Perhaps you will feel differently by and by. Now leave me in peace." Sheba's chin sank to her chest, and she was silent. They waited, but she did not raise her head again. After a while she began to snore.

"She is asleep," whispered Rowan.

"Asleep or pretending," said Strong Jonn in disgust. "In any case, there is nothing more for us here. We must go back. The others have waited long enough for us."

They left the hut and began to hurry toward the village.

"And we return empty-handed!" exclaimed Marlie. "With Rowan bleeding. Rowan, I cannot forgive myself for stepping aside and leaving you to be struck. I was taken by surprise."

"The old devil intended Rowan to suffer," said Strong Jonn grimly. "She was punishing me for laughing at her and telling her to beg his pardon. The fault is mine."

Rowan, trotting along beside them through the orchard, was feeling dizzy and faint, but whether this was because of the cut on his forehead or simply the terror he had felt in Sheba's cottage, he did not know. Her horrible warnings whirled around in his head, and her strange, droning chant seemed to have been burned into his brain. He could not forget it. "Seven hearts the journey make. Seven ways the hearts will break." He found himself repeating it under his breath, beating time against his leg with the stick he still held in his hand. "Bravest heart will carry on / When sleep is death, and hope is gone."

"Put it out of your mind, boy Rowan," said Strong Jonn uneasily. "Look ahead—the village lights. You will soon be home with your mother." He exchanged glances with Marlie. "And what she will say to me for bringing him home in this state . . ." he added in an undertone.

3 ⌒ THE HEROES

After inspecting the cut on her son's forehead, however, Jiller simply smiled and shrugged. It was nothing serious, she said, and could be attended to at home later. All children had to put up with such things at one time or another. Rowan knew that her words were for him as much as for Strong Jonn and Marlie. She was reminding him to be brave, as befitted a child of Rin, and not to fuss.

Rowan knew that Jiller worried about his nervousness and frailty. He had overheard her telling Strong Jonn so outside their house only a month or two ago. She tried to be patient, Jiller had said, but Rowan was so different from herself, and from his father, and even from sturdy little Annad, that it was sometimes very hard. She did not understand him. She wished his father was alive.

Rowan had crept away and scuttled upstairs to the room he now shared with Annad. He had lain on his bed for quite a time, not really thinking about anything, aware only of a dull ache in his chest.

So now he stood beside his mother with swimming head and burning eyes and said nothing. He longed to throw himself into her arms and cry for comfort, but there would be no comfort there. Only shame.

"I told you Sheba was a waste of time!" Bronden was saying, half in triumph and half in exasperation. "Now she has two of our best cheeses in her grubby paws, and we are none the wiser."

"Never mind," Allun said, shrugging. "We decided to try her, and try we did. Now a new decision must be taken. For we all cannot climb the Mountain. Who is to go?"

"I will go," shouted Bronden. She glared at them all, as though daring someone to oppose her.

"Why not?" Strong Jonn said. "No one doubts your willingness, your courage, or your right, Bronden. As, I presume, no one doubts mine. I, too, will go."

Rowan's heart felt as though it was being gripped

by an icy hand. He remembered Sheba's words: *The Mountain will not test your strength, Jonn. It will destroy it.* "No!" he gasped. His mother's hand tightened on his arm.

"And I," said Marlie firmly, her eyes on Bronden.

Val and Ellis had been talking quietly together. Now Val raised her gruff voice. "Until the mill wheel turns again, we have no work to do," she said. "So we will join you on the Mountain. Better that than sit idle, waiting."

"You could do a bit of housecleaning for a change," Allun teased.

Val stared at him coldly, while some of the other villagers exchanged amused glances. Everyone knew that Val and Ellis did not like anyone to make fun of their fussy housekeeping.

"This is madness," cried Neel the potter, unable to keep silent any longer. "This is no laughing matter! Bronden, Jonn, Marlie, Val, Ellis . . . the strongest of us all, going into the unknown!" He appealed to the crowd. "If they do not come back, these hotheads, how are we to survive? What will happen if the Zebak invade once more? Or if some other dreadful danger threatens?"

"Another dreadful danger does threaten, Neel," old Lann said. "Right now, as we stand here. Perhaps the most dreadful we have ever faced. To save the village from it, some of us must journey into the unknown. That is exactly why the strongest must be the ones to go." She turned to Jonn. "Still, I think the party is too small as yet. You need one more."

Allun stepped forward. "I agree. I will join the company to make the numbers even." He saw Bronden open her mouth to object and went on quickly, "Ah, Bronden, I know I am only half bred of Rin, and my strength may not match yours. But I am not quite a weakling. I have mastered, I think, all the skills the journey will require. And I have other gifts to offer, thanks to my father's blood. A cool head, for one. A good way with a campfire for another. And a stock of songs and jokes that will not go astray. Besides, with the millers absent and no flour to be had, how else will a poor baker occupy these next few days?"

"You could come and dig my garden, Allun," piped up Sara, his mother.

There was a shout of laughter from the people around. The old woman smiled. Only Rowan and Allun saw that her hands were gripping her apron, twisting the white cloth, and that her eyes were twinkling not with laughter but with unshed tears. She had lived long enough to have heard the old stories of the Mountain and to fear its power. And Allun was her only child.

But like a true daughter of Rin, Sara knew how to hide her feelings. Only once, many years ago, had she let down her guard. And that was when she had fallen in love with the man who became Allun's father, a laughing brown-eyed singer who came to the village one autumn with a troupe of Travelers. Rowan had heard the story many times, though the thing had happened many years before he was born, when his mother and father were children themselves. It was part of the village history and was repeated every time a tribe of Travelers came to camp nearby.

Rowan could imagine the shock it must have caused when it became known that Sara, the sensible village teacher, would leave Rin to marry a footloose Traveler. Most people were horrified and tried hard to make her change her mind. But she would not be persuaded, and when the Travelers moved on, she went, too, leaving the peace and security of her old home to wander with the man she loved and his tribe.

The people of Rin saw Sara a few years after that, when the Travelers chanced to come their way again. The small, cheeky-faced Allun was toddling after her by then, and her happiness was in her face for all to see. Some shook their heads and said her smiles would not last. And they were right, though not for the reasons they thought.

For then came the five-year War of the Plains, when again the people of Rin, the Maris folk, and the Travelers themselves were forced to join in battle against invaders from across the sea—their ancient enemy, the Zebak. As their ancestors had done before them, they at last drove the Zebak from their lands. But the battle was long and cost many brave lives. And one of these was Sara's husband.

Sara brought her young son back to the village after that. Without her man, the traveling life had no sweetness for her, and she wanted to settle again with her own people, in her old home. But home for Allun was the colored tents of the Travelers, the smell of campfires burning in the night, open plains, forests, and winding roads that seemed to have no ending.

Slender, dark-eyed, and curly-haired, Allun was the image of his father and very different from the tall, strong children of Rin. Under the teaching tree with Bronden, Jiller, Val, Ellis, and the others of like age in those days, he held up his head and smiled at their glances, nudges, and whispers. Outside school, though he worked hard to seem as like them as possible, he soon learned that his strength was no match for theirs and that his wits were his best weapon.

Rowan had often felt that Allun might be the one person in the village who understood how he felt, since he, too, was weaker, and different from the others. Not that Allun had ever said so. But when he visited the house with Marlie and Strong Jonn, he often joked with Rowan, and took an interest in what he was doing, and made excuses for his mistakes.

And now Allun, too, was to climb the Mountain Trying yet again to prove himself a worthy citizen of Rin. Jonn and Marlie were looking pleased, and Bronden was rolling her eyes at Val and Ellis, clearly not liking the sixth member of the party but unable to think of a good reason to deny him. Funny, easy-going Allun the baker was going to vanish with the others into the secret maze of cliffs and forests that rose above them. Once more Rowan remembered Sheba's mocking face.

"Ah, well, if you must go, you must! My weeds will have to thrive for another few days," old Sara was calling, smiling and flapping her hands in mock despair while her eyes still shone with tears.

"Bless you, Mother," said Allun. His tone was light, but the love and admiration in the words were clear for all to hear.

"Now," said Jonn hastily, for he was a man embarrassed by strong feelings openly expressed, "I suggest we go home and make our preparations for the journey. Then a good night's sleep should be had by all before the dawn is upon us. Agreed?"

The others nodded. The villagers called out their good-nights and began slowly to move homeward. Some felt comforted because something was being done to solve the problem that had come upon them so unexpectedly to spoil the calm progression of their days. Some felt excited, even envious, at the thought of the great adventure awaiting the chosen ones. But many, like Neel, went to their beds that night with heavy hearts because the leaders and heroes of the village were going on a dangerous quest for their sakes and might never return.

When Annad had finally fallen asleep, exhausted by the excitement, Rowan lay awake in his bed, looking out of the window at the huge bulk of the Mountain. The moonlight was very bright, but the Mountain loomed black against the sky, secret and full of mystery. Jiller had cleaned the cut on his forehead, but his head still ached, and Sheba's jeering words of warning tormented him.

He tried every way he could to turn his thoughts to pleasant things. To Star, to the new calf soon to be born in the herd, to the taste of cool blue juice from the hoopberry press. And to memories of the mother of his babyhood, a gentler, happier Jiller, singing to him. But always, just as he was about to fall asleep, the other, darker thoughts came creeping back and made him afraid to close his eyes.

Finally he did sleep, a shallow doze filled with nightmares. He was back in Sheba's hut. But now its four walls were made of rock, dripping with water and slime. And Sheba was huge, her nose long and pointed, her hair greasy gray tails swinging like thick ropes around her grinning face, her eyes red and piercing. Strong Jonn and his mother stood there with him, but they made no move to help as the Witch bent toward him, closer and closer, till her face was all he could see and her breath scalded his cheeks. "If you are the only one afraid, skinny rabbit, you are the only one with sense," she croaked. And she opened her mouth to scream with laughter, but she had no tongue, and the inside of her mouth was as yellow and smooth as cheese.

4 ∞ SEEING IS BELIEVING

Rowan woke and lay panting and shuddering, soaked in sweat. He had no idea what time it was. The dream had seemed to take hours, but it might only have been seconds. Annad slept peacefully on, her mouth slightly open, one hand curled around her soft bukshah toy. She at least was having no bad dreams. But the thought of going back to sleep was terrifying to Rowan. He threw back the covers and leaped out of bed. It was very cold. The cool night air was blowing in the window, and his sleeping shirt was wet through. He peeled it off and quickly began pulling on the day clothes he had left in a pile on the floor when he changed for bed.

Underneath the clothes was the stick Sheba had hurled at him. He had carried it home, unthinking, and brought it to his room. He picked it up and slid his fingers up and down its length. It was a good stick: straight and thick and so smooth it might have been polished, except for one little pointed bump in the middle. That was possibly what had cut his forehead, Rowan decided, pushing the soft pad of his thumb against the bump. It was hard and sharp enough.

Then the bump moved! It slid forward under his thumb. And the stick began to peel!

Rowan gasped as the smooth surface beneath his fingers came away in a fine, single sheet. He pulled at the sheet, fascinated, as more and more of it unrolled. Then he realized that the "stick" was not a stick at all. It was a tightly rolled piece of parchment. The little bump in the center had been the catch that held it closed.

With a glance at the sleeping Annad, he hurried to light the lamp. She would not wake, and he had to look more closely at this strange thing he held in his hand. For even in the dimness he could see that the parchment was not blank. There were pictures on it, and lines and words. He had to see what they were.

He spread the parchment out on the wooden floor and weighted it on all four corners with his shoes and Annad's to stop it curling up again. Then he carefully put the lamp beside it and looked.

It was a map of the Mountain, with a pathway marked in red. Rowan clapped his hand over his mouth to stop himself calling out. Sheba had played a trick on them. She had pretended to let them down, knowing all the time that Rowan was carrying away just what they needed. Knowing that they might never discover what she had given them. How she must have laughed to herself at Strong Jonn's disgust and Marlie's disappointment.

Rowan rolled up the map tightly again and fastened the clasp. He pulled on his shoes. Then he stood in the middle of the bedroom, his thoughts whirling.

"Rowan! What are you doing?" He spun around to meet his mother's startled eyes. She gaped at him from the doorway. He blinked at her. Like him, Jiller was fully dressed as if ready to go out.

"I . . ." Tongue-tied, he held out the rolled-up map. "I had a dream, and—"

"Oh, Rowan," Jiller sighed in exasperation. "These nightmares! What am I to do with you, my son?" For a moment Rowan thought he saw her lips tremble. "And now, this morning—" She broke off and put her hands up to her face. When she lowered them, she was calm again. "If we wish to bid the Mountain party farewell with the rest of the village, we must go soon," she said. "They leave at dawn. Put down that stick and gather Annad's clothes. I must wake her." She moved toward the little girl's bed.

"Mama . . ." In his confusion Rowan used the babyish word without thinking. He saw her brow crease and heard her quick indrawn breath of irritation.

"Mother." He went on quickly and so loudly that Annad stirred and began waking of her own accord. "Mother, I have the map. The map of the Mountain!"

"He has the map of the Mountain," Jiller said again to Strong Jonn, ignoring the exclamations of the crowd. Her cheeks were pink with excitement, and her hood was flung back over her shoulders. She looked very beautiful to Rowan. And perhaps she did to Strong Jonn, too, for he was looking at her admiringly.

"Then quickly, let us see!" demanded Bronden, stamping her tough boots in the cold. "But I cannot believe this! Why would the old woman try such a trick? Are you sure the boy is not playing the fool?"

"Of course not," snapped Jiller, taking the map from Rowan and passing it to her. "See for yourself!"

Bronden unrolled the parchment and stared at it for a moment, her breath making little puffs of mist in the cold morning air. Then her mouth turned down at the corners, and she passed the parchment to Jonn and Marlie.

"Well?" Allun, standing beside Rowan and Jiller, was feverish with curiosity. "What is it? What has the boy found?"

Strong Jonn turned the parchment around to face them. It was completely blank.

"But—" Rowan burst out, "it was there! A drawing of the Mountain. And words and arrows . . . and a track marked in red, leading to the cloud and above it! It was!"

Bronden sniffed and jerked her head toward the empty sheet still dangling from Jonn's hand. "Seeing is believing," she said, turning away. "Small boys should learn that it is a big mistake to try playing tricks on their betters to gain attention."

"Maybe you were dreaming, Rowan," said Allun, patting him on the shoulder. "Too much cheese at dinner, eh? This happens to me sometimes. Things seem to be real—"

"This *was* real," Jiller broke in. She was frowning,

staring at the parchment as if even now she could not believe her eyes. "Rowan held it up to me. I saw it myself. Am I, too, playing a trick on my betters, Bronden?"

There was an embarrassed pause. Strong Jonn bit his thumb thoughtfully. Then he passed the parchment back to Rowan. "If Jiller and Rowan say the map was there, I believe them," he said. "But the fact remains that now it is not. Perhaps Sheba wished to build our hopes, then send them crashing down."

Jiller smiled at him gratefully.

"That would be very like her," agreed Marlie. "She—oh!" Her jaw dropped, and she pointed at Rowan. "Look! Look!" she gasped.

Rowan, red-faced and startled, found the eyes of the villagers upon him. People were exclaiming and staring. What was happening? What had he done now? It took him a moment to realize that they were not looking at him. They were looking at the parchment in his hand. He glanced down at it, and the stab of shock he received was immediately followed by a rush of relief and joy. For the map was slowly reappearing. Shapes, words . . . and finally the red-dotted path, winding upward.

Strong Jonn held out his hand. "Rowan, give it to me," he commanded.

Eagerly Rowan surrendered the parchment. Jonn

took it and held it up. There was a buzz of excitement and then a groan of dismay from the villagers. For as they watched, the lines and arrows were fading. In moments the parchment was blank and clean again. Jonn passed it around. The people stared at it as it went from hand to hand, unchanging.

"It is witchcraft!" exploded Neel, thrusting it back to Strong Jonn as if it were poisonous. "Sheba is toying with us."

"I fear she is," said Jonn slowly. "And it is a dangerous game she plays." He looked at Marlie. "I am very much afraid that Sheba's idea is to make me eat my words," he said to her.

He put the parchment back into Rowan's hands and watched gravely as once again marks, shapes, and lines appeared on its surface, faint at first, but growing clearer by the second.

"What does this mean?" cried Jiller, clutching her son's shoulder.

Strong Jonn hesitated. "Last night, angered by something I told her, Sheba said of Rowan: 'It would do you no harm to be guided by him.' I believe that out of spite she has bewitched the map so that it only reveals its secrets in Rowan's hands."

"You are right." Marlie was thinking aloud. "She threw it at him last night. She intended him to discover it. She intended that this scene we have just witnessed should be played out." She paused. "Sheba wants the boy to join us on the Mountain."

"No!" The word burst from Jiller before she could stop it. She bit her lip and composed herself. "I mean," she went on carefully, "Rowan is young. Too young to be of use to you. And he has the bukshah to see to. He cannot go."

"Of course he cannot!" agreed the teacher, Timon. He pushed his way to the front of the crowd. "And I have the solution to this little dilemma. Rowan can hold the map while I copy it, with my own ink on my own paper." He spread out his hands. "It may take an hour, and Rowan's arms may tire, but it will be worth it to him. Rowan can then go home to bed, fortunate boy, while you poor fools go off for your little stroll."

"Yes!" Marlie exclaimed. "We will beat Sheba at her own game. She forgets we are not bukshah, to be led about so easily."

But Sheba had forgotten nothing. For no matter what Timon did, he could not copy the map. Whenever he tried, the pens he used and discarded one after the other skated across the copying paper as if it were greased with butter, though they worked perfectly if he tried to draw anything else. After half an hour he had not succeeded in producing one useful line. Finally he threw away his last pen with a grunt of disgust and sat back on his heels in a mound of screwed-up paper.

"Enough!" said Jonn. "We were going without the map before. Nothing has changed. We go without the map now." He nodded to Rowan, carefully avoiding Jiller's eyes. "We thank you," he said. "For at least we have seen glimpses of the way. We will remember much of it, and this will help us. Go home now, with your mother."

"But this is senseless!" snapped Bronden. "The map will ensure our success and safety. We must take it with us. And if the map and the boy are joined, by whatever trick, we must take the boy with us, too. Anyone can take his place with the bukshah. His attachment to them is foolishness in any case."

"We agree with Bronden," said Val. Her brother, beside her, nodded. "The village depends on this. There is no room for faintheartedness here."

"The boy cannot come," insisted Strong Jonn. "The danger is too great. And he is too young."

"Or is it that his mother is too beautiful?" remarked Bronden pointedly. "And your heart is ruling your head, Jonn of the Orchard?"

Jonn's face flushed scarlet. Rowan felt Jiller's arm stiffen and saw her lift her chin while two spots of bright color began to burn in her cheeks.

"Mama, what's the matter with Jonn?" whispered Annad, pulling at her mother's skirt. "Why is he all red?"

Jiller did not reply. Rowan looked from one face to the other in the crowd and slowly, with a sinking feeling, the truth came to him. There were other children here of his age. If this had happened to any of the others, there would be no argument. It would be taken for granted by Jonn and Timon, by their parents, and by everyone else that they would go. And they would want to go. It would be the greatest adventure of their lives, their chance to prove themselves heroes.

It was because he was . . . the way he was, that Strong Jonn was taking this stand. Because—he saw it now—Strong Jonn loved his mother and was trying to save her from shame and pain.

Rowan began to quiver. Sheba's words rang in his ears. *The Mountain will not test your courage. It will destroy it.* Why had she done this to him? If the Mountain could destroy the courage of one such as Strong Jonn, who feared nothing, what could it do to Rowan of the Bukshah, who feared everything?

He was filled with dread, loneliness, and shame in equal parts. He could not bear it. He could not bear the rueful eyes of the villagers upon him. They, too, must be thinking: Why him? The most disappointing child in the whole of Rin. By what unlucky chance was he their chosen savior when all he could do was let them down?

He turned toward his mother, ready to hide his face in her skirt, and just at that moment a picture flashed into his mind. He saw himself standing in the bukshah fields, with Star's warm muzzle bent to his hand and the other beasts grazing around him, huge, calm, and trusting.

He had never disappointed the bukshah. He had never let *them* down. In the frosty early mornings or in the heat of the sun, when they were injured, or giving birth to their calves, or when they needed comfort as the Dragon roared, he had been there.

Now they needed water. They would not expect him to fail them. To them he was not an undersized, scared weakling. To them he was leader, guide, and friend. They trusted him absolutely. The thought flowed through him like warm, rich milk.

He raised his head and looked straight at Strong Jonn. "I will go," he said. The map he held fluttered in the little breeze that always came before the dawn. "I will go with you to the Mountain."

5 ∽ THE MOUNTAIN

They had been walking beside the dry bed of the stream for hours and had left the village far behind. Looking back, Rowan could no longer see even the tall stone walls of the mill, the highest building, because the trees had screened it from view.

In front of them, like a massive wall, rose the Mountain. In another two hours, the others said, they would reach it. The map showed clearly that they must begin their climb at the place where the water gushed from its underground tunnel to form the stream. There they would rest for a while and consult the map before going on.

Rowan was very tired. The bag he carried was dragging at his shoulders, and his back and legs ached. But he knew he had to keep walking and not complain. The others were trying to make it easy for him to keep up, but he could tell that the slow pace was irritating at least Bronden and Val. It was hard to tell how Ellis felt because he rarely spoke at any time. Even when they had passed the mill and the great wooden wheel lying motionless in the millrace, its own channel on one side of the dry streambed, he had said nothing. Only looked, then turned his head back toward the Mountain.

Rowan watched him now, striding at the head of the group. He carried his pack and the extra weight of a heavy rope, a small ax, and their supply of torches with ease. Close behind him walked his sister.

They were a strange, silent pair. Rowan had heard Jiller say to Strong Jonn that it was as though they lived in a world of their own, a world inhabited by only two people. They seemed as hard and immovable as the stone walls of their mill. They were about the same age as Jiller, and Rowan had taken them for granted as he grew up. They were just part of the normal day-to-day life of the village for him, like the other adults he had known since babyhood. But lately he had come to realize that Val and Ellis really were unusual. And that his mother and people like Strong Jonn and Allun thought so, too.

Behind Val, a head shorter but stocky and determined, tramped Bronden. Marlie came next, smiling
occasionally at Allun, who was swinging along
beside her, whistling and singing as if he was on a
country jaunt.

They had put Rowan second last, with Strong
Jonn bringing up the rear. Every now and then Jonn
would speak to him. "All well, Rowan?" he would
call heartily. Or: "Nearly there now, my friend."
Rowan would nod and mutter an unwilling answer.
He knew Jonn didn't really care how he felt. He just
felt responsible for him.

Jonn was good-natured and agreeable to everyone. It was his way. And he had always been pleasant to Rowan. But that was different from liking. He
cared for Annad—you could see that. But with
Rowan he never really relaxed. He tried too hard to
be nice. You don't have to try when you really like
someone. Rowan knew that. And sometimes Jonn
called him skinny rabbit and laughed at him for
being afraid of things.

Jonn was talking to him now because of Jiller.
Rowan had heard his mother whisper, "Take care of
him," as she said good-bye to the big man before
they left. And Jonn had taken both her hands in his
and said: "I will, Jiller. By my life, I promise I will
bring him home to you."

Remembering this, Rowan felt a flash of resentment. What right had Strong Jonn to look at his mother like that? What right had he to hold her hands as if he were more to her than her dead husband's friend? It had been a shock to him, there in the market square, when he realized that Jonn might feel more for his mother than simple friendship. It had been horrible to think that he might even plan on becoming her husband one day. No one could ever take his father's place, thought Rowan bitterly. No one.

He stamped along, staring straight ahead. And Jonn *should* feel responsible for this mess, he thought. It was Jonn's teasing that had angered Sheba so that she had made Rowan the keeper of the map. It was Jonn's fault that Rowan had been forced to become the weak, unwanted seventh member of this party.

At that, Rowan's thoughts changed direction, and his anger cooled. He wondered whether Jonn and Marlie had remembered Sheba's words: *Seven hearts the journey make. / Seven ways the hearts will break.* They had said nothing, but surely they must have thought about it, as he had. A shiver ran down his spine. There was no way that Sheba could have known the number of travelers in advance. Unless she really had had a vision of the future as she lay back in her chair, her eyes half closed. And if that part of the prophecy had come true, what of all the rest? Rowan bent his head to watch the ground under his feet. He did not want to look at the Mountain.

As the last hour's tramping drew to a close and the rocks of the Mountain's foothills loomed large and sharp, the sun was already warm on Rowan's back. For some time now he had managed to stay on his feet only by thinking of the bukshah. While Jiller had been loading his pack for the journey, he had slipped away to the fields to say good-bye. He had found the beasts swaying anxiously in the green grass that still surrounded the muddy drinking pool.

"We are going to help you," Rowan had told them as he moved from one to the other, stroking and patting, drawing in the familiar, warm animal smell of them. "Soon there will be sweet water again. It won't be long."

Last of all he had come to Star. He put his arms as far as they would reach about her neck and laid his head on her shaggy wool. "Good-bye, Star," he had said. "Wait for me. I will bring back the water. I will not fail you."

He knew Star could not understand his words, but she had grunted and snuffled to him as if comforted just by the tone of his voice.

"Annad and Mother will see to you while I am gone," he had told her. "If Dawn has her calf while I am away, they will help her. They promised me."

One final hug, and he had to go. But Star's trust and strength stayed with him, even when his knees trembled with tiredness and his breath shuddered in his chest.

"Yo, Ellis!" Strong Jonn's shout broke into Rowan's daydream. Allun and Marlie came to a stop in front of him. He stumbled to a halt and looked up. Before him rose a cliff of rock. Beside him the dry streambed had become a deep round hole, still puddled with a little muddy water. There was a black opening in the cliff just above the hole. Dying weed and moss crusted its smooth edges. So this was where the water came from.

"The water usually gushes from there," Strong Jonn was saying to Val and Ellis, pointing to the opening. "When it is running as it should, you cannot stand here without being soaked by spray."

Bronden clambered down into the empty pool and walked busily around in it, kicking at the soft mud. Then she bent over the rock to look up into the opening in the cliff face, as though hoping to find an answer there.

"Sheba said the problem was at the top of the Mountain," said Marlie, who did not seem to be able to stop herself from being irritated by Bronden. "There is nothing to see down here."

"There is no harm, I suppose, in looking for myself, Marlie the weaver," Bronden retorted. She rubbed her hand against the rock, feeling up into the hole in the cliff as far as her arm would reach. "A round tunnel. The bottom, walls, and top are polished smooth," she reported, and wiped her slimy hands against her clothes before climbing back onto the bank. "All the sharp edges have been worn away by the running water, no doubt."

"As one would expect," snapped Marlie.

Rowan sank down on the grass. His knees would not hold him any longer. He pulled off his heavy bag and fumbled in it for his drink bottle.

"Drink a little, but not too much," Allun warned, kneeling beside him. "We do not know how long our supplies may have to last. We may not find water on the Mountain."

Rowan swallowed a mouthful of warm, metal-tasting water. It was delicious! He could have drained the flask easily. But he forced himself to replace the cap, and as he did so, tears sprang into his eyes. He was so tired. And the real journey had not even begun.

The other members of the party threw down

their bags and stretched. Then, one by one, they, too, flung themselves down on the grass.

"The map, Rowan," urged Allun. "Let us see it now. But hold on to it all the time, mind you. The coming and going of the figures upsets my stomach."

Rowan took the map from his pack and unrolled it on the grass, weighting the corners down with stones. The others gathered around.

"We are here, you see?" said Strong Jonn, his finger hovering over the surface. "And according to the red markings, we must start climbing at just this point. The track goes up past the cave from which the stream flows and continues until the Mountain levels and the trees begin. Up there." He pointed to a waving mass of green leaves high above them.

"A steep climb," grunted Val. "The boy will have trouble."

"Then we will have to help him," said Strong Jonn cheerfully.

Allun was puzzling over the map. "What are these white patches?" he asked, waving a finger over several places on the parchment.

Marlie frowned. "They are all beside the path. Six of them, in all. Could it be that Sheba has erased some things of importance to trick us?"

"I would put nothing past her," said Strong Jonn.

"But after all, it is the path that is most important, and that at least is clear."

"Quite right," put in Bronden, stretching and yawning. "It is pointless to be concerned with anything other than the task at hand."

But Rowan stared at the white patches on the map with a growing sense of anxiety. Why had he not noticed them before? Now that he had seen them, they jumped out at him. Blank spaces almost evenly spaced along the path, the last at the very top. Blank spaces on a surface otherwise completely covered with color and line. What did they mean? The first space was at the point where the path entered the trees. They would find out what it meant soon enough.

"We go through the forest at first, it seems," Bronden was continuing. "A flat walk, due west. That should be easy enough, though of course with the boy it will take us longer." She sighed heavily and returned to the map.

"The directions are clear. Where the forest trees end, we turn northwest and move across this lower ground. A short distance, it should not take long to cover. And so on, and so on, up to the top. Simple! I have a compass, fortunately. And so, I know, do Marlie and Jonn, for we traded for them together on our last trip to the coast." She turned to Val and

Ellis. "You really should take your turn on the market trips, my friends. So many interesting things to see and useful things to trade for."

Val shrugged. "The mill must keep working, Bronden. We cannot close it down to gallivant whenever we please."

"But one of you could go, and one could stay," suggested Allun lazily, chewing a blade of grass and blinking up at the sky.

Val went very still. "That would not suit us," said Ellis flatly. "It is not our way."

"You never go to the coast either, Allun," Marlie pointed out. "You always say you are too busy. You are as bad as Val and Ellis!"

Bronden opened her mouth to say something, then thought better of it. "In any case," she remarked instead, after a moment, "the compasses are a marvel. The Maris folk use them when sailing the open sea. How much easier than that will our task be, for we have landmarks to follow also. We will be home by tomorrow midday, mark my words."

"If it were so simple, we would not have needed to bring the map with us, Bronden." Marlie leaned forward. "The Mountain is a dangerous place. A place to fear. You should take nothing for granted."

"I take nothing for granted, Marlie the weaver, as you know, except the evidence of my own eyes," snapped Bronden. "And if you fear, you should not be of this party. It is bad enough that we must drag the boy along, quavering in his boots."

"Do not forget, Bronden, that you were the one who insisted upon that," said Strong Jonn sharply.

Bronden shrugged and turned away.

"It would be better," said Allun mildly, "if we put aside our differences." Then he sat up and widened his eyes. He held out his hands, making them tremble violently. "And if fear is the issue, I, for one, am terrified!" he squeaked. He threw himself back onto the grass, wagging his head and chattering his teeth.

Strong Jonn and Marlie laughed, and even Rowan managed a smile. But Val and Ellis stared silently first at Allun and then at each other. Bronden snorted.

"Well, if Allun can be revived from his terror, I think we should begin," Marlie said, pulling a thick rope from her pack. "We will climb with ropes, will we not? I may not feel the fear of which I am accused, but I do not fancy a fall on those rocks all the same."

When food was scarce in Rin, Rowan had had to climb trees, bending the leafy branches down to meet the snuffling, eager mouths of the hungry bukshah. But he clung dizzy and pale to even the lowest boughs. He had no head for heights. The climb that followed was to him like the worst of nightmares.

A rope attached him to Marlie, Allun, and the other climbers above and to Strong Jonn below. When he slipped, as he did over and over again, his light body, weighed down by his pack, swung sickeningly into space, as far as the rope allowed. The sky spun above him; the ground spun below. His own terrified scream echoed in his ears. His ribs were crushed by the rope that saved him. And then his body swung back against the rocks with a bruising thud. And he had to climb again.

This was bad enough. But worse was the fear that one of the others would prove as careless as he. If Jonn slipped, the weight might pull them all to their deaths on the rocks far below. If one of the others slipped, even Jonn might not be able to hold them.

Sore, trembling, and aching in every muscle, Rowan struggled on. And when at last they dragged him over the top of the cliff, and he fell to the ground, sweating and panting, the world swam red before his eyes for a moment before he fainted.

6 ∽ THE FOREST

Star was licking Rowan's cheeks and forehead with her rough, cool tongue. Rowan smiled. "Stop it, Star! Leave me be," he mumbled. He rolled his head from side to side on the grass.

"He is babbling," someone said in disgust.

The picture of Star slowly dissolved. Rowan opened his eyes and found himself staring into the serious face of Strong Jonn. For a moment he hesitated. Then, with a wave of bitter disappointment, he realized where he was. Not home in the bukshah fields with Star, who loved him, but on the Mountain with Strong Jonn, who disliked him, Marlie and Allun, who pitied him, and Bronden, Val, and Ellis, who despised him.

"He is babbling," Val repeated impatiently. "By my life, how we are burdened by this weakling. Look at the sun! It must be nearly eleven."

Jonn threw aside the damp cloth with which he had been bathing Rowan's face. "He is awake now," he said bluntly. "And weakling or not, he fought that cliff gallantly, Val the miller. He fought it to exhaustion." He stood up and walked away, arching his cramped back.

Rowan lay still, looking up at the sky. His body felt heavy, but his head felt very light. There was a soft ringing in his ears. Val was right. The sun was high. He must have been lying here for a long time. Sleeping. Dreaming of home, like a small child. His face began to burn, and he struggled to sit up.

"Easily, easily, boy Rowan." Allun grinned as he knelt down beside him and supported his back. "We must crawl before we can walk. Have this." He held a flask to Rowan's lips, and Rowan swallowed gratefully.

"When you are feeling better," Allun went on, glancing meaningfully at the others, "we will move on, into the forest. Here!" He dragged Rowan's pack toward him. "You can spend your time usefully by holding the map for us while we look at it once again."

"We have seen the way we must go," said Bronden. "We do not need the map."

"Ah, youth, youth! You must not forget that I am three years older than you, Bronden." Allun was smiling. "And my poor memory is failing fast."

Rowan knew that Allun was only giving him something to do while he rested, but he slid the map from his bag and unrolled it slowly. It would not hurt to study it again. His eyes traveled along the red-dotted line, past the sketched-in streambed, the hole into which the water usually fell, the opening in the cliff, the cliff itself, the entrance to the forest beside a high, pointed rock not far from where they now sat, the path through—

Rowan blinked, and looked, and blinked again. He tried to speak and almost choked.

Allun looked at him quickly and then glanced at the parchment. He exclaimed under his breath. Then, "Jonn!" he shouted.

Jonn spun around and ran back toward them, while the other members of the party craned their necks to look.

Rowan was pointing wordlessly at the map. At the place beside the beginning of the forest path where once there had been a clear white space, there were six lines of black writing.

In a low voice Allun read the words aloud:

"Let arms be still and voices low,
A million eyes watch as you go.
The silken door your pathway ends,
There fire and light will be your friends.
Then see yourself as others may,
And catch noon's eye to clear your way."

"What nonsense is this?" demanded Val. "Who has been playing the fool?"

"No one has touched the map, Val," retorted Marlie. "The words have appeared since we last looked at it."

"That is impossible!" said Bronden. She bent over the map, squinting at the words as though to find a clue to how they had come there.

"It matters not a jot where it came from," cried Allun. "The question is, What does it mean?"

Strong Jonn cleared his throat. "Whatever we are dealing with here," he said, "it is certain that the words have not come to us by chance. They give us instructions, and a warning."

"The words suggest we not fling our arms about or speak loudly," Allun remarked. "That is clear enough. I shall follow that advice to the letter."

"That may prove difficult for you, Allun," said Marlie dryly.

"The words also mention noon." Strong Jonn was

unsmiling. "I suggest we begin our forest journey as soon as we can. It will be noon in about an hour, by my reckoning."

He held out a hand to Rowan and hauled him to his feet. "Roll up the map, and stick it through your belt for now, boy," he said roughly. "My load is unbalanced, I find, and I need to carry your pack as well as my own to even the weight, if you do not object."

He did not wait for an answer but swung both bags onto his shoulders and began striding toward the pointed rock. The others hurried after him. Rowan, no longer weighed down by the pack on his back, found he was able to keep up quite easily, despite his bruises.

They paused at the pointed rock and peered between the first trees. Sunlight filtered through rustling leaves and lay in pools on the forest floor. There was a rough winding path in front of them, soon lost to view behind the undergrowth.

"This looks pleasant enough," said Allun. "Shall I lead this time? The gravity of the task may help me hold my tongue as the verse commands. Stranger things have happened."

"Then lead by all means," grumbled Bronden. "Any peace from your infernal chatter will be a blessing."

They moved into the forest. Rowan noticed that all of them, whatever their feelings about the map's instructions, kept their arms close to their sides. And no one spoke. In a few minutes the path had twisted and turned so that they could no longer see the clifftop from which they had come.

As they trudged deeper into the forest, the trees around them became bigger and closer together, tangled with vines and surrounded by straggling bushes. The light became dim. And the silence! Rowan, keeping close behind Marlie and listening for Strong Jonn's firm step behind him, thought that he had never experienced so silent a place. Where were the birds? And the crickets and lizards and other small creatures that usually inhabited woods like this?

Then he heard it. A faint twittering sound was floating down the path from somewhere ahead of them. A large colony of small birds, by the sound of it. Rowan was familiar with all the birds of Rin, but this sound was like nothing he had ever heard before. These little creatures must belong to a breed that did not stray into the valley. They would not be nesting at this time of year, but still he looked forward to seeing them fluttering and hopping around. His spirits lifted at the thought of it.

The twittering grew louder and louder. Allun began to walk faster, as if he, too, was interested in what was ahead. Soon he had left Marlie behind.

She clicked her tongue and hurried to join him. Rowan, stretching his legs to keep up, tried to peer around Marlie's shoulder as the path turned once more. And so he stumbled and nearly fell as she gasped and cannoned into Allun, standing still and almost invisible in the dimness. The cheeping sound was deafening now.

Strong Jonn grabbed Rowan's arm and steadied him, frowning as Val, Ellis, and Bronden bumped into him in their turn. And still, Allun did not move.

"Allun, you blockhead, what game are you playing?" Bronden barked.

The twittering stopped abruptly. And a rustling, creeping, whispering sound took its place.

Allun looked back at them, his face creamy pale in the dim light. But he did not answer, only moved his head, very carefully, from side to side.

And then they saw what he had seen. On both sides of the narrow pathway. Spiders. Thousands of them. Huge black velvety spiders, as big as Strong Jonn's hand, crawling over vast webs of white silk that draped the trees so thickly that the bark and leaves were hidden. Their eyes were shining. *A million eyes*. Rowan's skin began to creep. They were going to have to walk between these crawling webs, the gigantic spiders listening for them, reaching out for them.

"Ugh!" Rowan heard a strangled gasp from somewhere behind him. The spiders froze and then
began moving again, in the direction of the sound.

Strong Jonn reached over Rowan's shoulder and
pushed gently at Marlie, as a signal to move on. She
pushed Allun in her turn, and he began easing forward, making as little movement as possible. But
they had only gone a few steps before again there
was a shuddering groan behind them, and Val was
pulling at Strong Jonn's sleeve.

"Ellis," she breathed. "He . . . cannot."

Jonn, Rowan, Marlie, and Allun turned incredu-
lously. Beyond Val's worried face they could see the
massive form of Ellis, his clenched fists crossed over
his chest. His face was gleaming with sweat. He was
panting and trembling, and every now and then a
low moan slipped from his lips.

"Spiders," breathed his sister. "He cannot abide
them. From a child he could not. At home not a
speck of dust or a dry leaf may lie in a dark corner
in case a spider seeks its shelter. The smallest of
them is terror to him. And these . . . are beyond
anything—"

"Ellis?" whispered Strong Jonn urgently. "Come,
man. It is not far. They are not on the path. If we
take care—"

"No-o." The sound bubbled from the big man's

lips. Abruptly he turned and pushed past Bronden, nearly toppling her off the path and into a web. He tottered back the way they had come. Then he rounded the bend, and they could see him no more. But they heard the sound of his feet . . . running. Running out of the forest.

"Go on!" whispered Val, her voice fierce with worry and shame. "Go on! He will not return."

Silently they obeyed. After a few minutes the twittering sound rose again. The spiders were communicating once more, slowly rubbing their great ribbed back legs together like poisonous crickets. The noise was strange and horrible to hear now that they knew where it came from. Rowan crept along behind Marlie, breathing in shallow gasps, making himself as thin and small as possible. Trying not to look from side to side. Trying not to think of the sticky white curtains that swathed the trees, the huge, crawling spiders and their million eyes so close.

To allow himself to speak or cry out would be to attract the spiders again. To touch one of the strands of thick white silk would be to call them, running, to him. He had seen enough insects caught in webs to know that. He must go on walking and force down the fear. He must think, remember the last lines of the verse: *The silken door your pathway ends, / There fire and light will be your friends. / Then see your-self as others may,/And catch noon's eye to clear your way.*

The silken door . . . noon's eye. It must be nearly noon now.

He jumped nervously as Strong Jonn's hand touched his shoulder. He looked up. They were in a small clearing. Before them was the silken door. It was a huge gleaming white web, so thick that he could not see through it. Its surface was scattered with twigs and leaves caught in its sticky threads. It stretched from one side of the path to the other, blocking it completely. And all around it crouched hundreds of spiders. Waiting.

Allun turned carefully to face his companions. "What now?" he mouthed.

"The verse," breathed Marlie.

"The verse has no meaning," hissed Bronden. "Cut through the web and be done with it, Allun. Or if you do not have the stomach for it, let me through and I will do it myself!"

The spiders rustled and moved in the web.

"No!" whispered Strong Jonn. "Not while the spiders hang about the silk in such numbers. As soon as we touch the web, they will be upon us. We cannot risk that."

"They may be quite harmless," said Val.

"Or they may not," answered Marlie. "As Jonn

says, we cannot risk it. We have already lost one
member of our party."

"What then?" Bronden was angry. Ellis's flight
from the forest had been a great shock to her. How
could such a big, strong man have such a childish
weakness? She was baffled by it. She took care not
to look at Val. How shamed she must feel.

The light changed. From directly above them a
ray of sun penetrated the gloom of the forest,
bathing them in warmth. The spiders around them
began to chitter and creep back.

"They do not like the light," Rowan breathed.
"The verse said it—'Fire and light will be your friends,'
it said."

"Fire!" whispered Bronden. "Throw a torch at the
web!"

"Ellis was carrying the torches," said Val dully.

Allun felt in his pockets and pulled out his tinderbox. "Who has something that will burn easily, even
for a brief time?"

"Do not make any sudden movements," warned
Strong Jonn, his eyes on the spiders.

Marlie slipped her hand into her jacket pocket.
She pulled out her compass, a comb, a mirror—and
a handkerchief. She held the handkerchief out to
Allun. He knotted it loosely and struck flame from
the tinderbox.

"Ready?" he asked. Then he lit the cloth and threw it straight at the center of the white barrier.

The silk sizzled and shrank as the handkerchief blazed. The spiders shrieked and scattered. But only for a moment. Within seconds, before even one of the party had taken more than a step forward, the flame had died down and the spiders were back. A hole gaped in the web now. But amid the smoke still rising from its blackened edges hundreds of spiders were crawling. And more were on their way.

"They are spinning," gasped Allun. "Already! They are mending the hole."

"We must drive them back!" Strong Jonn looked around desperately. "There must be a way."

"They do not like the light," Rowan said again. "They do not like the sun."

"We have no materials to make a torch here, Rowan," Marlie answered. "We have nothing that will make a light that will burn long enough to hold the creatures at bay."

But Strong Jonn had grasped Rowan's shoulder. "Rowan, the verse. Say the last lines again."

Rowan repeated in a low voice: " 'Then see yourself as others may, / And catch noon's eye to clear your way.' " A thought struck him, and he looked quickly at Marlie.

" 'Noon's eye'—the sun!" Allun squinted upward

at the glare. "But the sun is falling here, where we stand. The web is in shadow."

"What is it, Rowan?" asked Marlie, staring at him. "Why are you looking at me?"

"The mirror," whispered Rowan. "Your mirror. In a mirror you see yourself as others may. And the sun—"

"Yes!" Strong Jonn clenched his fists. "But quickly, quickly! Before the light goes. We have been here too long."

Marlie handed over the mirror. Jonn held it in front of him, twisting it until it threw bright reflected sunlight onto the web. The spiders scuttled away from their work around the hole, shrinking back into the shadows.

"Give it to me!" cried Val. She snatched the mirror from Jonn's hand. She jiggled the glass, caught the sun, and dazzling light danced around and around on the silken door. She pushed Bronden ahead of her. "Go!" she shrieked. "Go now!"

Rowan ran with the others, his eyes fixed on the hole in the web and the glimpses of green beyond. Already the dancing light was fading. He reached the net and leaped through, while a million eyes glowed angrily in the shadows, cheated of their prey.

7 ~ DREAMS

Strong Jonn and Bronden hit the ground beside Rowan and rolled to their feet.

"Val!" called Jonn, stumbling back toward the hole in the web. "Val! Now! Before the sun moves on!" He peered through the opening. "She is just standing there!" he muttered in amazement. "She keeps looking back along the path, after Ellis."

"Jonn, make her come!" shouted Allun. "The sun will soon—"

"Val!" roared Strong Jonn, cupping his hands around his mouth. "You are needed. You must come. Quickly!"

There was a cry from the other side of the web and the sound of running feet. And then Val was hurtling through the black-ringed hole, hitting the ground with a thud, and Strong Jonn, Marlie, and

Allun were stamping, stamping the grass all around her as crawling spiders fell from her clothes and hair.

Val sat up, brushing feverishly at her face, her shoulders, the back of her neck.

"No, no!" exclaimed Marlie. "All is well, Val. There were only a few of them, and now they are dead."

Val looked around her cautiously, taking in her surroundings. Then she opened her clenched fist and looked at the mirror. Amazingly, it was still in one piece. "It did good service, but I could only keep the light on the web while I remained in the sun," she said. "I leaped from a distance, but some of the creatures had already returned to the hole before I reached it." She passed the mirror to Marlie and sat with slumped shoulders, staring into space.

"We appear to be safe here." Allun waved an arm at the surrounding trees. "From the spiders at least. Their territory seems to end with the silken door. What other surprises this forest has to offer, I cannot guess."

"If I recall the map correctly, we are nearly at its end," Bronden answered. "So I suggest we move on now and rest and eat when we are free of it. It is an unwholesome place."

In silent agreement, they set off again. Due west,

along the path. They were six now, instead of seven, and all felt this keenly. Ellis had barely spoken ten words during the journey, but the absence of his looming figure among them made their group seem very much smaller and weaker. His sister was particularly affected. It was as though half her strength had been drained, and she walked like one who was ill or exhausted.

In barely five minutes they noticed the trees thinning. In another five they had left them behind and turned northwest as the map directed. Although the Mountain still rose steeply before them, they were moving down instead of up. The grass grew green and thick now, and the ground softened with every tread.

"Let us stop here," said Strong Jonn. "It seems we are moving into a low area that may be marshland. We will eat in more comfort out of the damp."

Rowan sat down thankfully. Jonn tossed his pack to him, and suddenly he realized just how hungry he was. He pulled out his water flask and bread and cheese and started eating ravenously. His mother had packed this food for him in their kitchen at home this morning, he thought with wonder. Only this morning! It was hard to believe that he had been away from the village for so short a time. So much had happened to him that it seemed days, not hours, since he had patted Star and murmured to her, since he had hugged Annad and kissed his mother good-bye.

The walk from the village, when he had felt so strange and shy. The terrible climb up the cliff. And then the forest. The spiders, twittering, crawling . . . Ellis's face rigid with fear before he turned and ran. Rowan shuddered. The bread and cheese lay tasteless now in his mouth. He felt like spitting it out but instead took a sip of water and forced himself to swallow.

Sheba had said this was how it would be. She had said the Mountain would break their courage, and their hearts. Well, it had broken Ellis's, in a way no one could possibly have predicted. He was gone, leaving six hearts to carry on. Would they break in their turn? Would Rowan's be next? And if the journey was itself so filled with danger, what of the journey's end—and the Dragon?

Rowan shivered again. He must not think of that. One step at a time, or his fears would overwhelm him. One step . . .

The map! Rowan pulled it from his belt and unrolled it. Half in excitement, half in dread, he looked at the second blank space.

It was filled.

Nothing here is as it seems;
Dreams are truths, and truths are dreams.
Close your ears to loved ones' cries;
Die if you believe your eyes.
Bind with ropes your flesh and blood,
And let your guide be made of wood.

Rowan stared. "The map . . ." he began timidly. "A message—"

In a flash Jonn was behind him, looking over his shoulder. Allun and Marlie, too, came running. Bronden joined them more slowly, grumbling a little. And Val remained where she was, slumped with her back against a rock.

"This verse is more confusing than the last!" exclaimed Allun.

"Yet we know the last was important to us," said Marlie. "And this must be, too." She read and frowned. " 'Close your ears to loved ones' cries.' " She glanced at Allun. "We are going again into danger, it seems."

"We knew from the start," said Strong Jonn, "that every part of this journey would be so." He rubbed his chin thoughtfully. " 'Bind with ropes your flesh and blood,/And let your guide be made of wood.' So the party leader is of importance this time. We had better decide what is to be done about that. What does 'made of wood' mean?"

"Wood is hard," said Marlie. "Hard . . . smooth . . . cool . . ."

"Bloodless," Allun put in helpfully. "Unfeeling. Incapable of pain."

"Strong," added Bronden. "Sturdy. Natural. Of the earth."

"Yes." Strong Jonn rubbed his chin again. "The least emotional of our party, then. The one who can most resist the cries of others. The one with fewest ties to flesh-and-blood things. That person should lead us."

"Well, it is not I," said Allun decidedly. "And of course it is not Rowan. And I would venture to say, Strong Jonn, that it is not you. Not these days, at any rate." He shot a sly look at Rowan, who turned his head away. He did not want to think about Strong Jonn and his mother. Not now. *Not ever*.

"I believe that of the three remaining, I am the most likely," said Bronden. "For I have no family, no loved ones. I work alone with wood day in, day out and find it pleasing. I believe only what I see with my own eyes. I will lead."

And so it was decided.

Thirty minutes later, fed and rested, they were traveling once more, walking northwest by the compass. There was no obvious path now. Pleased to be leading, Bronden was in a good mood for the first time since the journey began. Val walked behind her, still strangely silent, her feet dragging. Allun and Marlie came next. Then Rowan with Strong Jonn, who was again carrying the boy's pack "to balance the load." All of them stopped obediently when Bronden decreed, to help cut the limp, spiky tips from the pine-smelling trees that were growing along the way. Bronden said that later the stems could be bound together to make long-lasting torches to replace the ones that had been lost when Ellis fled.

They were still walking downhill, and the ground was becoming wetter underfoot. The green grass had disappeared, and their boots were beginning to sink slightly into the mud.

Allun sniffed the air and wrinkled his nose. "Swamp!" he said in disgust.

The trees they pushed through here were different again—dark-leaved and still. Fat white roots slid up from their damp, twisted trunks into the air. Clumps of bright fungus stuck out from their barks like tongues. The mud grew softer. Rowan's boots splashed with every step he took.

And then came the mist. Bronden bent over her compass, frowning in her efforts to guide their way

as it swirled, thick and yellow-white, around them.
It swirled around the trees, too, and rose like steam
from the glossy mud and clumps of reeds that
stretched away on all sides. As the minutes passed,
it grew thicker.

At last it seemed as though they were enclosed in
a still, secret world. A world of mist and mud. The
only sound was the squelching of their feet as they
plodded on. Before them, behind them, and around
them swirled the mist, changing shape and direction by its own will, it seemed, for not a breath of
air stirred the trees.

Then, to his left, Rowan saw something moving.
Something large and dark. He slowed, straining his
eyes to see through the mist that twisted and billowed, disguising the shape. The shape of—

Rowan cried out. It was Star! Star, heaving and
panting in a wallow of mud that was sucking her
down, down. The mist cleared, and he could see her
rolling her eyes in panic, thrashing her neck from
side to side in the sticky, suffocating swamp.

Without a thought he leaped to her rescue,
ignoring Jonn's shout of surprise. He could hear her
now, bellowing in fear, calling to him for help. "I am
coming, Star!" he screamed.

But the mud was sucking at him, pulling him
down. He could not find a place to put his feet.

There was no firm ground. He was sinking, sinking into mud that had no ending. He cried out again and beat at the mud with his arms. And still Star called to him. And the mud rose to his waist, his chest—

"I have him! Pull!"

Strong Jonn's voice woke Rowan from his dream of terror. Strong Jonn's arms caught him under the armpits and dragged him, with a horrible sucking sound, from the mud. And Bronden and Val, holding Jonn's ankles, hauled them both back to safety. They fell in a heap on the oozing ground.

"Fool of a boy! What idiocy is this?" roared Bronden.

"Star!" cried Rowan, struggling in Strong Jonn's arms, sobbing and beating at Strong Jonn's wet, muddy chest. "My Star, my bukshah! She is out there. Oh, help me! She is drowning. She is dying! Listen to her!"

"There is nothing there, Rowan." Strong Jonn spoke slowly and loudly. "Nothing! Think, little one, think! How could Star be here? It is impossible."

Rowan's struggles slowed. He fell silent. He looked out to the spot where Star had been. The mud lay still and untroubled. The mist swirled above it as before. He rubbed his eyes. "It . . . seemed so real," he faltered.

"You—" Bronden began, leaning over him menacingly. "Real or not, would you endanger our lives and our quest for the sake of a dumb beast? What value is there in a bukshah's life, compared with a human one? What madness—"

"Leave the boy be, Bronden," Jonn broke in. "You have reasons for what you say, I know. But not all share your views."

"The map," Marlie added quickly, as Bronden drew a sharp breath. "The map warned of this. It spoke of dreams that seemed true and loved ones who called to you. There are spirits abroad here who do not wish us well."

The map! Rowan felt anxiously at his belt. The map was still there. Covered in sticky mud, but at least not lost forever.

"Spirits!" spat Bronden. "You have been spending too much time with your half-Traveler friend, Marlie the weaver. Do not listen to his tales. You are a daughter of Rin and should be a person of sense." Bronden scowled and turned away.

Allun and Jonn exchanged glances. "Let us get on," Allun suggested. "We have lost time. And we will have to lose more in due course, while Rowan and Jonn dry their clothes. Which are"—he held his nose—"rather in need of attention, in my opinion."

"Let us take great care where we tread," warned Strong Jonn. "The mud is a snare. We may not be so lucky next time."

They moved along at a snail's pace, the mud dragging at their boots. The mist thickened around them, filling their mouths and noses with the taste and smell of the bog. Rowan hung his head as he walked. The wet filth sticking to his clothes and filling his shoes weighed him down. And still his head was full of Star. He dared not look up in case he saw her again, struggling hopelessly in the swamp. He wondered why Bronden had been so angry with him. Surely she could understand. . . .

He felt, rather than saw, Marlie begin to flick her hands and rub at her cheeks and the back of her neck. "I can feel—someone is touching me," she gasped, glancing behind her. "Fingers. Cold fingers, on my face and neck, and—"

"It is only the mist, Marlie," soothed Allun. "Only—" Suddenly he stopped walking. His neck jerked, and he, too, looked behind, gazing over Strong Jonn's shoulder. The others turned curiously to see what he was staring at. But there was nothing there.

"What . . . ?" Allun's mouth had dropped open. He began to walk back the way they had come, pushing past Jonn and Rowan, looking into the mist. "How . . . Mother? Mother! Wait!" His feet squelched in the soft, sucking mud.

"No, Allun," screamed Marlie. "There's no one there! Jonn, stop him!" Then she shook her head violently. "Oh! Stop it! Stop touching me!" She slapped again at her neck and arms and rubbed at her face.

Lost in the mist ahead, Bronden cried out, just once.

Jonn caught at Allun's jacket and pulled him back. Allun turned on him angrily. "Leave me be, Jonn," he shouted. "It is my *mother*, you fool! She is calling me. She is lost in the swamp. I must go to her." He began to struggle, trying to wrench away from Strong Jonn's grip, throwing punches at his face.

"No, Allun, no!" shouted Jonn, shaking him. "It is a vision! A vision! Your mother is at home, man!"

"What is happening?" wailed Val from farther up the path. "Why don't you come? Oh, my life, help! Ellis! Oh, Ellis! Marlie! Jonn! Help me! Bronden— Bronden is . . . and I can't hold her. Help!"

8 ⮑ FLESH AND BLOOD

Marlie and Rowan ran toward the sound of Val's voice. Jonn followed, dragging Allun, who was still struggling but starting to look confused instead of angry.

They found Val lying facedown in a clump of reeds, her feet on solid ground, her body in the mud, her arms around Bronden's waist. And Bronden was fighting her. Silently and determinedly fighting to be free, stretching her fingers out to something only she could see, while the swamp pulled her down.

"She suddenly called out and plunged away into the mud," gasped Val. "I cannot pull her back. She will not listen to me. Oh, if only Ellis were here. I—I cannot think without him."

Marlie pulled a coil of rope from her pack. "Hold

me, Rowan," she called, and flung herself down to lie beside Val.

Rowan held Marlie's ankles and watched her stretch across the reeds, reaching for Bronden. Marlie was tall, but not as tall as Val. As she crawled farther out into the mud, Rowan was pulled forward, until he, too, was lying on his belly across the pathway. His muscles strained as Marlie pushed her hands under Val's and looped the rope around Bronden's belt. Val, too, groaned. She had been bearing Bronden's weight for so long. She would not be able to hold on much longer.

"Back! Rowan, try to pull me back now," shouted Marlie. "Can you do it?"

Rowan heaved with all his might, but Marlie was heavy, and her ankles were slippery with mud. To his horror he felt his hands beginning to lose their grip. "Jonn," he shrieked in desperation. "Help Marlie! I can't—"

"Marlie!" There was a scuffle behind him. Then two slim, strong hands had come down on top of his own, and Allun's voice was calling, "I have you, Marlie," as he heaved her to safety, with the rope that was Bronden's lifeline clutched in her hand.

It took all three of them to haul Bronden back, while Val lay exhausted on the ground and Rowan stood helplessly by. The mud was holding fast to its victim, and Bronden herself was fighting them. Even when they had her safe at their feet, she was moaning and crying, trying to crawl back into the ooze that had nearly swallowed her forever.

"Minna," she was weeping. "Minna, Minna, Minna!"

"Who is Minna?" Rowan whispered to Strong Jonn. He had heard the name before, but he could not think where. "Who did Bronden see?"

Jonn was shaking his head sadly, looking down at the crying woman. "I had forgotten little Minna," he said. "I had forgotten all about her until Bronden became so angry with you for thinking of the bukshah. And I think, except in a secret part of her mind, Bronden had almost forgotten her, too. But this place . . ."

"When we were all children, Rowan," said Allun, "and I was still new to Rin, Bronden had a friend. One friend—Minna, the keeper of the bukshah in those days. A little girl as quiet and gentle and fearful as Bronden was loud and bullying and fearless. They were never apart. For Minna, there was only Bronden and the bukshah. For Bronden, there was only Minna."

"I remember Minna," said Marlie softly. "And so

would your mother, Rowan. We all went out looking for her—even the children—the night she disappeared."

Bronden groaned and looked up at Val, who was
bending over her anxiously. "Minna is here, Val,"
she croaked. "I saw her. I heard her voice. I felt her
hand on my face. But Val"—her strong face crum-
pled, and tears fell from her eyes—"Val, she is still a
little girl. She has never grown up. She has been
wandering here all these years, all alone. Why did
you not let me go to her?"

Strong Jonn knelt down beside her. "Minna died,
Bronden," he said gently. "They found her bones, at
last, and the bones of the calf she was trying to
save, in the old mine shaft. You remember."

Rowan stared. Minna had been quiet and shy,
like him. Minna had died, seeking a lost bukshah.
Was that why—

"We do not know that that was Minna, with the
calf," Bronden moaned. "We do not know for sure. I
have always wondered. . . ."

Jonn stroked her forehead. His face was full of
pity. "Minna is dead, Bronden. Minna is safe and
resting in the graveyard. The spirits of the swamp
played a terrible trick on you, to make you leave the
firm ground. As they did with Rowan and his bukshah. And tried to do with Allun and his mother."

"I do not believe in such things." Bronden looked around her with terrified eyes. "And yet you must speak truly, for Minna cannot be ten years old still. But I saw her. I felt her. I heard her." She gripped Strong Jonn's hands. "Jonn! Do not let them touch me again! Do not let me hear them! I could not bear it." She struggled to her feet. The mist billowed around her, and she started like a frightened animal.

"Come along, Bronden," said Strong Jonn, still in that gentle voice. "Come along." He began to lead her on.

"No!" Bronden dug in her toes, her eyes black with fear. "No! I cannot!"

"Bronden, you must come!"

"No!" She tore away from him, panting, then turned and began to run back the way they had come, her thumbs over her ears, her hands blinkering her eyes.

"Bronden," shrieked Val. "Come back!"

But Bronden did not turn or hesitate. Soon she was out of sight.

Now we are five, thought Rowan.

"The spiders!" Val groaned. "She will not be able to go through the forest!"

"She has the branches she cut to make torches," Allun said. "Once she is out of here she will stop and bind them, for the fear will die in her, and she will regain her senses. From this side she can burn the silken door to nothing and leap through in safety. She is strong. She will be safe. She will return to the village, like Ellis."

Val began to shiver. She looked shrunken and exhausted. "Ellis has not returned to Rin," she whispered. "He is waiting for me, at the edge of the forest. I feel it. I know it. I have known it all along. Never have we been apart so long. Never in our lives, since we were in the cradle. I have tried so hard not to think of it, but—"

"Let us go," said Strong Jonn heavily. "We will tie ourselves together. None of us can be trusted not to stray."

Bind with ropes your flesh and blood.

But tears were rolling down Val's plain, muddy face. "I cannot go farther," she said. "I knew it when I called to Ellis as Bronden struggled in my arms. I am sorry, so sorry. But I cannot go on with you." She buried her face in her hands. "You will not understand. You will think ill of me. I do not blame you. But I cannot go on alone. Half of me is missing. Ellis is waiting. He needs me, and I must go to him."

She turned away. "I have torches to make also," she said. "I will move fast and catch up with Bronden. We will go together."

Rowan, Jonn, Allun, and Marlie watched silently as she trudged away, shoulders bowed. She did not look back.

"It is true," said Marlie at last. "It was as if half of Val departed when Ellis did. She struggled bravely, but in the end she could not carry on without him. It is strange. They both seemed so strong, as though nothing could touch them."

Four, thought Rowan. There are only four of us now. So soon.

"The Mountain is doing its work well," said Strong Jonn, echoing Rowan's thoughts. "And there is yet far to go."

Allun smiled wearily. "All the better, then, that those who are friends continue together. Come. Let us go."

"And, Allun—sing," added Marlie. "For once I wish to hear nothing else."

They looped Marlie's rope around their waists and bound themselves together in a line: Jonn, Rowan, Allun, and Marlie. They trudged on, looking neither left nor right, keeping their eyes to the ground, their ears filled with Allun's singing. His voice was sweet, but it sounded small and sad in the mist, and they took little joy in it.

"It was fortunate that you regained your senses,

Allun the baker, in time to prevent me from sinking in the mud and taking poor Rowan with me," remarked Marlie lightly, after a time.

"I heard Rowan's voice calling your name," said Allun, shaking his head. "And it was as though I was waking from a dream."

There was a shocked yell from Strong Jonn at the head of the line. He staggered backward, pulling one wet and muddy leg from the treacherous ground into which it had plunged. "The northwest path has failed," he called. "I cannot tell how deep the bog is. We will have to find another way."

He felt cautiously around him. But wherever he turned, the mud sank beneath his feet.

"What are we to do?" cried Rowan.

"The map's warning said, 'And let your guide be made of wood,'" Marlie began hesitantly. "We believed this to mean that the guide should be a person who would not feel too deeply about others." She thought for a minute. "But perhaps the words have a different meaning altogether. Perhaps they mean exactly what they say and were intended to help us at just this moment."

And so it was that the map's instructions were finally understood and carried out. They went back and cut the straightest branch they could find from one of the trees. They measured it against Rowan, the smallest of the party, and marked it at his shoulder height. And this branch, this wood, became their guide.

Jonn plunged the branch into the mud ahead of them. Where it came to rest on firm ground, and the mud reached a point below the mark, they stepped forward. Where it sank so deep that the mud rose above the mark, he tried again and again until a safe stepping place was found.

One step at a time they struggled forward, wading often up to their chests, in thick, sticky mud. Progress was painfully slow. And all the time the yellow-white mist floated about them, and sometimes shapes flitted just within their sight, and voices whispered. But they looked only forward, and closed their ears to the moans and cries that tempted them, holding fast to the rope that joined them one to the other.

Finally there came a time when on every side the wood sank so low that the mark was covered. Then Allun and Marlie shouldered Jonn's load, and Jonn took Rowan upon his back. And again they pushed forward, feeling their way, veering always to the northwest, till at last the mud began to firm beneath their feet, and the ground began to rise, and they knew that the dreadful journey was nearly at an end.

Staggering and exhausted, they climbed out of

the swamp and mist, past the twisted, dark-leaved trees, onto land where grass grew again. Up and up they crawled, to where the air smelled sweet and the sun shone. And there they fell to the ground at last and slept.

9 ∽ MOVING ON

Rowan woke shivering. The sky was orange and red around the cloud-covered mountaintop, and the air was growing chill. Jonn, Marlie, and Allun were still asleep, sprawled around him on the ground. All of them, even Strong Jonn, looked younger and more helpless like this. Their clothes, like Rowan's, were still damp and stinking from the swamp. Their hands and faces were streaked and filthy; their hair was soaked and caked with mud. How different was this small company from the one that had started out so bravely this morning. And how differently did he feel about his place in it.

Rowan watched the three adults sleeping and wondered at the feeling of affection for them that welled up in him. Before, though he had known them all well from his earliest childhood, he had been afraid of them. Now he trusted them. Not just to look after him but also—almost—to like him. He thought about this with surprise.

Marlie opened her eyes, blinked sleepily for a moment, and then saw him watching her and smiled. She sat up and ran her fingers through her sticky hair. "We had better wake the others," she said. "And light a fire. It seems to have been decided that we spend the night here."

Later the four of them sat around the blazing fire, feasting on toasted bread and melted cheese, sun-dried fruits, honey and oat cakes, and Solla's best hard brown toffee. It was dark now, and cold. The moon shone white in the star-filled sky, behind a hazy veil of cloud.

While they ate in the bright circle of light, Allun, Marlie, and Jonn talked of the village and told tales of times gone by and things that made them laugh. They could have been sitting beside Jiller's hearth in Rin.

Rowan sat and listened to them as he did at home and wondered why things suddenly seemed so nat-ural and relaxed. Then he realized. It was because Bronden, Val, and Ellis were no longer with them, and Allun had let down his guard. He still chatted and joked as usual, but his mouth had no bitter twist to it, and he was often content simply to sit quietly, poking lazily at the fire.

Rowan had heard Jiller say that when they all were children, she had decided that Allun's joking and playacting formed an armor stronger than Val's and Ellis's iron muscles or Bronden's bad temper. And in a way, although Allun was grown up now, Rowan could see that the armor was still kept at the ready. And needed to be since it was clear that for some villagers, like the three who had left them today, Allun would never be one of them. He would never be quite accepted, however much he wanted to be and however hard he tried, because of his Traveler father.

Rowan, watching Allun's lean brown face in the firelight, saw that in a way he was caught between two people—in his own eyes, at least. This knowledge kept him on guard. But here and now, with friends he trusted, he could truly be himself.

Rowan listened as the others talked, feeling comforted by their presence. No one mentioned Bronden, Val, or Ellis. No one looked at the map as it lay spread out to dry by the fire. No one talked about the swamp or the spiders or the trek still to come.

But when the food had been put away, and they

had woven Bronden's green stems into torches for the following day, and the fire had burned down to glowing embers, the heavy darkness began to press in on them. Gradually they fell silent. Rowan wriggled uncomfortably. They had dried their clothes as best they could and combed out their filthy hair, but they could not wash. The water in their flasks had to be saved for drinking.

Rowan would have given much for a long, hot bath. Mother would smile at that, he thought. I usually complain about having baths. And at once a pang of loneliness stabbed through him.

By now Ellis, Bronden, and Val would be nearly home. They would surely not let darkness stop them. They would stumble into Rin at a time when people were thinking of putting out their lamps and going to sleep. Annad would be sleeping already, in the little room she and Rowan shared. Jiller would be sitting by the fire downstairs. Reading, maybe, or mending something. Would she be thinking of him? What would she feel when she heard of the others' return?

Allun glanced at his sad face. "The same moon is shining over Rin, you know," he murmured, pointing to the sky. "Think of that."

"It is not worth packing this last piece of toffee,

Rowan," said Marlie, holding out the package. "You could finish it for us, I am sure."

"The map should be dry by now. Do you not think so, Rowan?" asked Jonn casually, at almost exactly the same moment.

Rowan realized that all of them were trying to comfort him in their own way.

He grinned shyly at Allun, took the toffee from Marlie, and nodded at Strong Jonn. "I will look at the map," he said.

He brushed the dried mud from the parchment. With his finger he traced their path and found the place where they now camped. It seemed that they had completed about a third of their journey. From here they must turn due west again, climbing until they reached what looked like a steep cliff. There the red line rose abruptly. Rowan's heart sank at the thought of another fearful climb.

He looked for the third blank space on the map. There it was. Or rather there was the spot where it had been. He bent over the parchment and haltingly read the words in the dim light of the fire:

"Look for the hand that points the way,
And take the path where children play.
Then where the face with breath that sighs

Bends to admire its gleaming eyes,
Your way is marked by lines of light
That mean escape from endless night."

"Children!" exclaimed Allun. "Are we to find *people*
in this place? Ah, people mean water, Marlie! And
hot tubs to wash in. And soft beds. And bowls of
soup!"

"Perhaps," said Marlie. "But do not forget that
people can also mean weapons and fear of strangers.
They will be many, and we are few."

Strong Jonn looked up at the dark, silent Mountain. "If there is a village so near, it is well hidden,"
he said. "Still, we shall see. Let us rest now. We will
start at first light. It would be well to be early visitors if visitors we are to be."

Despite his tiredness, Rowan lay unsleeping for
some time after good-nights had been said. The
others lay quiet, Jonn and Allun rolled up like cater-
pillars in their blankets, Marlie lying flat with hers
flung over her. She would be cold in the night, he
thought. He himself was warm, and the fire was
banked up and glowing. But the words of the map's
verse ran around and around in his head, always ending in the same way, the same frightening way that
jerked him awake and started the process all over
again. *Endless night . . . endless night . . . endless night . . .*

* * *

He woke with a heavy head to the sounds of Marlie heaping earth on the fire and Allun whistling. It was still quite dark, but the sky had lightened, and somewhere birds were singing. Rowan thought of Star and the other bukshah, moving to the pool for their morning drink with Jiller and Annad. He imagined their bewildered snuffling sounds as they found the water even lower than before. They would be getting very thirsty now. They would taste the brown muddy stuff that was left, and then they would shake their heavy heads and paw the ground. And they would wonder where he was.

We are going as fast as we can, Star. Rowan closed his eyes and thought the words as hard as he could, as if by doing this he could make his message reach his friend. Soon we will be at the top of the Mountain. We will make the water flow again. Soon. . . .

Then he remembered, and his eyes flew open again, filled with horror. Tomorrow—or the day after—they would reach the top of the Mountain. And . . . the Dragon. His heart lurched, and he felt sick. So much had happened to him, he had been so afraid on this journey, that for a while he had actually forgotten his greatest fear. Until now. And then he thought of something else. Another day. Another dawn. And the Mountain was silent, except for the birds. Again the Dragon had not roared.

He was still considering this when they set off again, due west and climbing. "Allun," he said timidly, "do you think that the Dragon could be dead? Or gone to another place?"

"I certainly hope so," replied Allun cheerfully. "After thinking the matter over carefully, I have decided that I would prefer not to meet it."

"There was no sound from the mountaintop this morning," put in Marlie.

"No, nor was there last night," agreed Strong Jonn. He glanced at Rowan. "Many do say, of course," he added, "that there is no Dragon at the top of the Mountain. No one has ever seen it. We have no proof that the old stories about it are true."

"Bronden certainly did not believe in it," said Marlie.

Instantly the same thought entered everyone's mind. Bronden had not believed in anything she had not seen with her own eyes. And Bronden had found that she had been wrong. Very wrong.

Strong Jonn began to walk a little faster. He was carrying Rowan's pack again, but even without the extra weight Rowan had to struggle to keep up. After a while he had no energy to think of anything but the steep way ahead of him. As perhaps Jonn intended.

They pushed through some ragged bushes clustered at the top of the rise. Then Allun exclaimed, and Marlie muttered under her breath. Rowan looked up. Rising over the tops of the trees directly ahead of them was a sheer cliff of red-gold rock glistening in the first rays of the sun. He gasped for breath and stared at it, fascinated.

He realized that he had seen this place before, many times, while tending the bukshah at sunrise. But then it had been small and far away. Then, gazing up at the Mountain, he had seen a mass of green, then a strip of gleaming red-gold, then the cloud that hid the Mountain's tip. But now the cliff rose in front of him, and he could see that it dropped from the cloud like a wall, a wall almost as smooth and straight as the side of the mill of Rin.

He could not climb it. He knew he could not. The very sight of it filled him with terror. He pressed his lips together so that he would not cry out, and despair welled up in him. They had come so far, and fought so hard, only to be defeated by the Mountain at last. For it was not only he who could not climb this cliff. The closer they came to it, the more he could see that no one could climb it.

There were no footholds. There was nothing at all to cling to on that red-gold stone. Not a plant, or a hole, or a sharp piece of rock. Nothing.

"We have a problem," Allun remarked.

"So it seems," Strong Jonn said. He scanned the cliff with narrowed eyes.

"We should not despair," said Marlie, wiping the sweat from her forehead and shivering at the same time. The air was cold now, and a chill wind blew around them. "The way may be clearer to us when we arrive at the spot."

Allun and Jonn looked grim as they began walking once more. Rowan could see that they did not share Marlie's hope.

But when half an hour later they emerged from the trees and saw what lay at the foot of the cliff, they realized the wisdom of her words.

"A cave!" said Jonn. He peered inside the dark opening that was like a door in the rock. "A very deep one, too. Could it be—Rowan!"

They clustered around as Rowan unrolled the map. The red line moved upward quite steeply, that was true. But not as steeply as the cliff rose to the clouds.

"Wonderful!" caroled Allun. "An easy way. And indoors out of the weather, too!" He turned to Marlie. "What a relief!"

She forced a smile. "Indeed," she answered. But Rowan saw that her face had grown pale.

They lit one of the torches they had made the night before. It flared up and then settled to a slow and steady flame. Marlie led the way, holding the torch out stiffly, as they stepped into the cave.

Piercing shrieks greeted them. Shrieks and the flapping of a thousand leathery wings as bats in their hundreds, disturbed from their daytime rest, fell from the roof of the cave and wheeled around them, beating at their faces.

Shouting, they bent their heads and crouched on the sandy ground, their arms protecting their eyes. Rowan could hear himself screaming with the others. It seemed an age before the high-pitched screeching sound had died and the panic-stricken creatures had departed. Only then did Marlie, Strong Jonn, Allun, and Rowan rise slowly to their feet, breathing heavily as if they had been running. They looked at one another, and then Allun grinned. "Who was more frightened, do you think? We or the bats?"

Relieved laughter echoed on the stone walls. The torch flickered, casting high shadows.

"Look!" cried Rowan.

At the far end of the cave, by the side of a wide, arched opening that seemed to lead into yet another chamber, stood a tall, oddly shaped rock, all by itself. It was narrower at the bottom than at the top, and from it pointed a long, narrow finger of stone.

Look for the hand that points the way. . . .

Torch held high, they walked forward and through the archway, deeper into the Mountain.

10 ∽ ENDLESS NIGHT

It was dark, so dark. And very cold. Marlie held up the torch, and Rowan drew breath in amazement. Countless rainbow-colored spears of stone hung glistening from the soaring roof of the chamber. Strange, squat shapes rose from its floor in groups and lines. The cave was huge. He could not see its ending.

Jonn took a step forward, glanced at his compass, then hesitated. "The compass needle is wavering," he said. "Something is interfering with its workings."

"Metal in the rock, perhaps," suggested Marlie. The torchlight flickered yellow on her face. She fidgeted, moving from foot to foot.

"Perhaps. In any case it would be foolish to rely on it too completely. But without it, how can we find the path we are to take? We could so easily become lost in this maze."

" 'And take the path where children play,'" said Rowan. "This is what the map told us."

"It would be a brave child who would venture here," Allun observed.

Rowan peered around him, standing on his toes and craning his neck until he saw what he had been searching for. "I think, perhaps . . ." he began, and faltered. Perhaps he was being foolish. He did not want to lead them astray or be laughed at.

"Speak up, Rowan," urged Strong Jonn. "This is not a time for anyone who has any plan at all to hold his tongue."

"It—it may be the stones," Rowan stammered. He pointed. "Those stones that are smaller than the others. Over there. There is a space between them, like a path. And their shapes—"

"Of course!" Allun took the torch from Marlie and led them to the spot. Sure enough, two lines of the strange stones, bent and knobbly like children tumbling and crawling, climbed off into the darkness. Between them wound a clear, sandy path.

"So our way is marked for us," said Jonn with satisfaction, putting away his compass. "And now—"

"We look for a face that breathes with sighs and

has gleaming eyes." Allun laughed. "That should be interesting."

He led them up the path, the torch lighting the way in front of him. Looking back, Rowan saw the cavern receding into the darkness. *Endless night.* He shivered.

They moved on. Upward. Always upward. They were climbing through the center of the mountain. Rowan tried not to think of the tons of rock and earth that surrounded them, pressing down, cutting off light and air. If they were lost here, no one would ever find them. They would wander in the endless night until they died, and the Mountain would be their tomb. He pushed the fear down, but it grew and pressed on his belly and his heart, making it hard to breathe.

Higher and higher they climbed, through one chamber to the next. By their sides, the rocky children bent and stretched in a game that had no ending. The climbers said little, for the way was steep. The silence was as thick around them as the darkness. Rowan listened to the hissing of the torch, to his own breath, to Marlie's panting behind him, and the sounds of Jonn's boots crushing sand and hitting rock in front.

"Another cavern!" Allun's voice bounced back to them from walls they could not see. They heard him scrambling forward, and the torchlight disappeared. "The face!" he exclaimed. "The face is . . ." His voice trailed off.

"Allun, what is it?" shouted Marlie, pushing forward. "Allun, answer! Allun, bring back the light. We cannot see!"

"The face," he called. His voice sounded strange, as though he were choking. "It is here. Come. But slowly."

The torchlight reappeared, and cautiously they climbed toward it. Allun was standing by a wide gap in the rock. He did not smile as they reached his side but thrust the torch through the gap. "See for yourselves," he said. "But again, take care."

They squeezed through the opening into the cave beyond. Rods of white and yellow stone hung thickly from the roof, but the black and shining floor below the ledge on which they stood was as smooth as glass. Facing them, on the far side, was a wall of rock. A wall, with a bulging lump in the middle. A lump shaped like a face, looking down. They saw the twisted, rocky nose, swollen cheeks, slitted mouth, broad chin. And gleaming eyes that cast beams of light across the floor. *Your way is marked by lines of light.*

There was sound here, too. A sighing, whistling, breathy sound.

"It breathes," whispered Marlie. "The face breathes, as the rhyme foretold."

"A passage on that side must open to the air," exclaimed Jonn. "That is the outside air we hear, Marlie! We have climbed far in these caverns. We must surely be almost at our journey's end."

"I fear," said Allun, still in that strange voice, "that I at least am at my journey's end now."

He was standing with his back pressed against the cavern wall, and as they stared at him, he slid down until he was sitting on the ground.

"Allun, get up!" Marlie ordered. "What game are you playing?"

"I would not have come if I had known," Allun said wearily. "But how could I have known? Whoever would have dreamed it possible?" He rubbed at his eyes, shaking his head.

"Allun, we do not know what you mean! Come! We must move on." Strong Jonn frowned and turned away. As he did so, his boot kicked a pebble from the ledge, and it fell to the shiny black floor.

There was a splash, and the pebble disappeared. Ripples spread in silent, ever-increasing circles across the smooth surface of what they all had mistaken for solid ground.

"Water," said Allun. He looked haggard. "The

cave is half full of water. Deep water, for it is black and cold and you cannot see the bottom."

"So?" Marlie demanded. "So we put up with the cold and swim."

Allun raised his eyebrows. "But you see, Marlie, my dear, I cannot swim."

"*What?*" They gaped at him, and he stared back defiantly.

"It is not a skill the Travelers teach their young," he said. "The Travelers sensibly leave swimming to the Maris folk. After all, they are the ones who get their living from the sea and have webbed feet and hands to make the whole miserable business more efficient. The Travelers refuse to have anything to do with water in larger quantities than a tin tub will hold."

"But in Rin we *all* learn to swim," Rowan burst out. "We have to. As soon as we can walk, practically. We have to go to the coast or the river on the plain specially to learn." He winced, remembering those lessons in the river. He had learned to swim in the end. But he had not enjoyed it.

Allun smiled bitterly. "Ah, yes. In Rin it is different. In Rin you must have every physical skill, of course, or you are regarded as useless. Even if you live far inland. Even if you have to travel a day and a night to practice swimming, and may never swim from one year to the next, or ever again in your life, still you must be able to swim, as you must be able to climb, fight, run, and so on and so on. Such things, in Rin, are thought so important."

"They *are* important," cried Marlie. "A person must be prepared for whatever adventure he or she might meet. As we can see, right now, Allun!" She faced him despairingly. "So you did not learn to swim as a small child. That is unfortunate. But why on earth did you not learn once you arrived in Rin?"

Allun glared at her. "Was I not already a figure of fun and ridicule? I, the strange-looking, skinny Traveler boy who had never worn shoes and knew nothing of your village ways? At ten years old the taunts of other children are very hard to bear. Rowan will tell you that." He glanced at Rowan, who nodded silently. So he had been right. Allun *had* understood how he felt.

Marlie took Allun's arm. "I understand, Allun. But you could have asked about swimming lessons—"

He rounded on her. "No, you do not understand. Was I to make even more of a clown of myself by letting those bullies under the teaching tree know of my weakness? I could not teach myself in secret. There is no water in Rin but the stream and the buk-

shah pool. I would have had to ask to be taken to
the river on the plain for lessons with the three-
year-olds! How Ellis would have crowed over that."
He shrugged, twisting his face into a comical mask.

"And as you can imagine, the longer I waited, the
more impossible it became," he said. "Before I knew
it, I was that unthinkable thing: an adult of Rin who
could not swim." He smiled. "It did not matter, of
course," he went on softly. "It did not matter a jot.
Until now."

Strong Jonn shook his head. "There must be a
way," he began. "If you just—"

"Jonn, you must accept this, as I have. I cannot
swim. Not a stroke," said Allun firmly. "So if you are
thinking of helping this lame duck along, pulling
him by one useless wing, perhaps, think again. The
water is icy. You will have enough trouble keeping
yourselves afloat, without attempting to stop me
from drowning also. The ropes will not stretch
across to the other side. So put that out of your
minds as well."

"This is why you never take the chance to visit
the coast on market days, Allun." Jonn looked at
him thoughtfully. "I have often wondered. . . ."

"Well, now your wonderings are at an end." Allun
smiled, but he turned his head away.

Marlie bit her lip. "You cannot return to Rin alone

now, Allun," she burst out at last. "The swamp will surely be your death, without a partner."

"I have thought of this." Allun brushed at his coat, as though removing the dried mud that clung there was all that was important to him. "I will make camp beside the cave mouth. I will wait for you there." He laughed bitterly. "I had thought to be a hero of Rin. Show them what the half Traveler could do. Who would have thought that such a small weakness would be my undoing? And that because of my foolish pride, I would let down my friends?" He did not look at Strong Jonn. "I would give much for it not to be so. Forgive me."

Seven hearts the journey make. / Seven ways the hearts will break.

But Jonn put out his hand. "There is nothing to forgive, old friend. Wait for our return. Make more torches if you can find good wood. We will need them." He hesitated, then went on in a lower voice. He had turned his head away from Rowan, but Rowan still heard what he said. "If we do not return in three days, Allun, you must wait no longer. You must find your way back to Rin somehow, to those who love us. Better that they hear the worst than that they do not hear at all. Is this agreed?"

"Agreed." Allun took Jonn's hand and squeezed it warmly.

"Let us go then," said Marlie. Her eyes were full of tears. She threw her arms around Allun. "We will be back," she whispered. "Take care."

"And you, Marlie."

Jonn, Rowan, and Marlie stripped off their boots and outer clothes and stuffed them into their packs. Then, shivering, they entered the water and began swimming.

It was, indeed, bitterly cold, so cold that Rowan's flesh first stung and then grew numb. The water flooded his mouth, harsh and sour. Across the black pool they crept, sidling like crabs along the lines of light, striking out with their right hands, holding their packs with their left hands so that they dragged along behind them, half in and half out of the water.

Nameless things brushed Rowan's feet and legs as he swam. He clenched his teeth at the thought of them but kept pulling himself along with an arm that grew heavier and slower with every stroke. Soon he was in agony, but worse than the pain of continuing was the thought of sinking down into this black, still hole, never to see light and air again.

Then his hand struck rock, and with a wave of relief he realized that he could stand. He looked up. The huge stone face was above him. Marlie was already climbing out of the pool, gasping and dripping. Behind him Strong Jonn heaved his pack out of the water as he, too, reached the shore. All of them turned and called to Allun, who was waiting anxiously on the other side. They were standing in shadow, so he could not see them, but he lifted the torch high in response to their shouts. At least he knew that they were safe.

Marlie bent and offered a hand to haul Rowan up beside her. His teeth were chattering so much that he could not speak. He jumped up and down to warm himself. With cold, clumsy fingers Marlie unbuckled his pack and pulled out the clothes he had stripped off before the swim.

"Take off your wet things and put these on before you freeze to death," she advised. "They are a little damp, but much better than nothing."

Rowan knew he couldn't do that. Not in front of Marlie. He didn't even undress in front of his mother anymore. He hesitated.

"By my life, Rowan!" Marlie exclaimed in amused exasperation, her own clothes clutched in her arms. "You have been menaced by giant spiders, nearly smothered in a swamp, and now half drowned and frozen, and you are embarrassed about taking your clothes off in front of me! Does that not seem ridiculous?"

"Not at all." Strong Jonn was grinning as he came up behind them. "I understand completely. Some things a man simply cannot do. I suggest you turn your back, Marlie. Then modesty can be preserved, and we can all get warm without delay."

11 ∞ THE SNARE

The torches were damp, but at last they managed to light one. The map, tightly rolled and securely wrapped in Rowan's clothes during the swim, had survived. John and Marlie crouched beside Rowan as he unrolled it and spread it out on his knees.

The red lines continued upward, twisting and turning. And in the next blank space, the verse Rowan had come to expect had appeared:

Left or right, which will you take?
For both of them your heart will break.
One is cruel, one is fair,
One a passage, one a snare.
Choose the one that hides the light,
And you will know your path is right.

They all looked up at the huge stone face. The gleaming eyes still cast their reflections over the water, and now that they were directly below them they could see that the eyes were hollow. They were entrances. To what? Which one was the door that led to the mountaintop? Rowan bent his head to the map again. The outline gave no clue. There was no marking showing twin passages. The only clues were in the verse.

"We will look at both and decide," Jonn said.

But when they had climbed the rocky face and peered into its eyes, they found that both caves looked alike. The walls of both were gleaming with a strange white-blue fungus that shone in the dark. Both were roughly the same size and shape, though the left was slightly higher and wider than the right. And from both came the sighing, breathy sound.

"What does it mean, 'One is cruel, one is fair'?" demanded Marlie. "They are both the same!"

"It says we should choose the one that hides the light," Rowan pointed out. "Perhaps we should try each of them in turn, to see where the torch flickers and dies."

Marlie moved uncomfortably, shaking her damp hair from her eyes.

"Agreed," said Strong Jonn. "We will first try the right-hand side. Who knows but that the last line of the verse is speaking the absolute truth, as it was in the swamp? It says, 'your path is right.' Perhaps it means just that."

They held up their torch to Allun and watched him raise his in answer and turn away to begin his lonely journey back to the cave entrance. Then they crawled up into the right-hand passage. It curved immediately, then curved again, and Rowan soon lost his sense of direction.

He could walk upright, but Marlie and Jonn had to bend their heads slightly, for the roof was low. They crept along, stumbling on the rocky floor, and the flame of the torch burned as brightly as ever. Then abruptly they came to a halt. In front of them the cavelike passage narrowed into a low tunnel, barely large enough to crawl through.

"That settles it," panted Marlie. "A snare if ever I saw one. Now we try the left. It was too much to hope for straight advice from Sheba."

The left-hand passage was easier to walk in. It was straight, at first, and larger than the other, and its sandy floor was smooth. But again the flame of the torch did not flicker. They walked on and on, turning corner after corner, in increasing puzzlement. The map had never failed them before.

The sighing sound was louder now. It filled their ears and whispered around them. And Rowan could smell something. A smell like damp, and mold, and cold, thick darkness.

At first he thought it was his imagination. Or the glowing fungus on the walls. He rubbed his fingers over it and smelled them. No. The fungus smelled of nothing at all as far as he could tell.

Strong Jonn, who was leading, slowed and finally stopped as the tunnel curved yet again.

"Go on, Jonn," called Marlie impatiently. "The faster we go, the sooner we will be out of here!"

"The tunnel is starting to go down quite steeply now," Jonn said. "The walls are smooth, with no handholds, and the sand will make it difficult for us to keep our feet."

"I do not like this place," Rowan murmured. "It looks fair, as the rhyme said. But it feels like danger."

One is cruel, one is fair, / One a passage, one a snare. . . .

Fear fluttered in his chest.

"Nonsense," Marlie said. "We have no choice. The other way is blocked."

"Not quite blocked," said Jonn, turning to face her. "There is room to crawl. It would be a cruel journey, but perhaps it is the way after all. The verse, remember, rhymes 'fair' with 'snare.' And I agree with Rowan. This place smells of death."

"You are both absurd!" Breathing in short, shallow gasps, Marlie pushed past Rowan. She grabbed the flaming torch from Jonn, darted around him, took two steps, and slipped. She scrabbled in the shifting sand, trying to rise, while the torch tumbled away from her down the slope, bouncing and turning.

Then it fell. Fell over the terrible drop that lay at the end of the tunnel. Fell and fell, while Marlie screamed. It hit bottom, finally, with a sickening crack.

They pulled Marlie up after them as they scrambled out of the tunnel, almost running, their hearts beating wildly at the thought of the fate they had escaped. One more minute, half a minute, and they, too, would have tumbled helplessly to their deaths over that underground cliff. Stumbling around the last bend, they fell on their knees at the tunnel entrance.

Marlie was shaking. "I am sorry. I am sorry," she said over and over.

Rowan, too, was trembling. Strong Jonn's weather-beaten face was drawn, but he roused himself with an effort. "Looking on the bright side, as Allun would say," he said, trying to smile, "at least we now know that the right-hand passage must indeed be the way. The tunnel is narrow, but if we leave our packs behind and take only what we can carry in our pockets, we can do it. We will have to crawl. And pray that it is not too long."

Rowan swallowed, thinking of that cramped dark hole they had seen in the right-hand cave. The idea of creeping into it, without any idea of where he was going or when the ordeal would end, was frightful. The red line on the map had been long. Very long. But he said nothing. The other way had been a snare indeed. It had nearly killed them. If they were to reach the mountaintop, they were going to have to crawl. So be it.

They lit another torch and edged across the right-hand passage. They entered it and followed its sharp bend as before, cutting themselves off immediately from the sight of the gleaming pool. Rowan drew a breath as he realized the truth. *Choose the one that hides the light.* This was the light the verse had meant. Not the torchlight, as they had thought, but the reflected light on the pool, cut off from their view by the turning of the right-hand tunnel, but clearly visible for minutes in the straight, fair left. They had misunderstood the words again. *Choose the one that hides the light, / And you will know your path is right.* The answer had been there, twice, clear for all of them to see. And still, they had blundered.

When they reached the place where the passage narrowed, Jonn, Marlie, and Rowan opened their packs and began transferring the most important of their possessions to their pockets and winding rope around their waists. It was clear that no baggage would fit through that tiny hole. As it was, Strong Jonn and Marlie would almost totally fill the space, and crawling would be slow and uncomfortable, with no turning back.

"Before we begin, we will eat," said Jonn, pointing at the food they had discarded. "We do not know when we will have another chance."

Rowan squatted on the ground and began to nibble at some bread and cheese. His stomach was empty, but it was churning, too, from fear and the bitter water he had swallowed in the black pool. He thought he had never enjoyed a meal less.

Marlie crouched over her pack, breathing hard. She ignored the food Jonn offered her. Rowan wondered whether she was ill. She had not seemed herself since they entered the caverns, except for the brief time when they were swimming. And now she was obviously in distress. Sweat was breaking out on her forehead, and she bit her lips as she pulled out her sleeping blanket and cast it aside with shaking fingers.

"Marlie." Strong Jonn's voice was low. She stiffened but did not raise her head. "Marlie," he said again. "It is the tunnel, is it not? It is the smallness of the tunnel that worries you."

"I am not afraid," Marlie said loudly. But still, she did not look up.

"Once we begin, Marlie, there will be no turning back," Jonn said. "If you feel you cannot do this, you should say so now. You have been uneasy ever since we entered the caverns. We all have seen that. You fear enclosed spaces."

"I do not! I am not afraid," Marlie said again. But her voice was thick. She threw back her head and looked Jonn in the eye. She was quivering with fear and tension. "I am ready," she said. "Let us begin."

She walked to the narrow opening and threw herself to the ground. Slowly she began to wriggle into the tunnel. They watched her head and shoulders disappear into the gloom, then her body, then her legs and feet. They felt her agony of mind as if it were a living thing. But they could do nothing but wait. Only when at last her strength broke, and she began to scream and gasp, to cry out to them and beat on the rocky walls, could they act. Only then could they pull her from the suffocating prison her fear had made and help her breathe again and still her cries.

"I thought I could defeat it," she sobbed. "I was

sure that this time, for such an important task, I could do it. But it overwhelms me, Jonn, as it always has." She buried her face in her hands.

"It is all right, Marlie. Marlie, be still," soothed Jonn.

"I do not like any shut-in place," Marlie whispered. "But when I cannot lift my head and shoulders, when I cannot move my arms freely, it is as if I cannot breathe. I cannot even wrap myself tightly in a blanket, for fear of it." She lifted her head and gulped at the air.

"So I saw, last night," said Jonn, smiling. "I thought perhaps you did not feel the cold."

"I nearly froze!" Marlie managed to answer his smile. "Jonn, I am so sorry. And Rowan . . . What will we do now?"

"We will do what must be done," said Jonn simply. "I will continue. You have a compass. Rowan has the map. You two will join Allun and together make your way back to Rin. If you follow the way we came with every care and remember—"

Marlie stared at him in horror. "But you cannot go on alone! Jonn, you cannot!"

"Marlie, I must. You know I must."

"No!" Rowan heard his own voice, loud in the echoing space of the cave. He could feel his face burning. "You cannot send me home. I have the map. You need the map. There are two blank spaces left. Two verses of warning still to come. You need to know what they are, Strong Jonn. You must take me with you."

"I cannot do that, Rowan." Jonn shook his head.

"I will not go back," cried Rowan. "You cannot make me." He ran over to the narrow passage entrance and sat down in front of it. "I must hold the map for you," he said. "I must find the water for the bukshah. I promised them." He set his chin.

Jonn stared back at him in helpless silence.

Marlie half smiled. "It seems you have met your match, Strong Jonn. With the son as well as the mother." She regarded Rowan curiously. "Who would have thought it?"

Jonn hesitated, then gave in. "Very well," he sighed. "So what will be, will be, and Sheba is to have her way." He put a big hand on Marlie's shoulder. "Good-bye, Marlie. And good luck on your journey home. Remember all we have learned. This time you will face the dangers well prepared. You will survive. Tell Allun that we four will meet again, in Rin." In two strides he was at Rowan's side. "Come then, before either of us changes his mind, skinny rabbit. You first."

"Take care," called Marlie as they disappeared

into the tunnel. "Take care, Strong Jonn and Rowan of the Bukshah."

Her voice echoed in the cave behind them, then faded into the silence.

Now, thought Rowan in the darkness, we are two.

12 ∽ BRAVEST HEART

Rowan was crawling with his eyes shut tight. He had found that this was better than facing the sighing blackness ahead. His hands were bleeding, grazed and cut by the rock. His legs ached with weariness. He could hear Strong Jonn pulling himself along behind, groaning with the effort as he struggled against the walls that pressed against his broad shoulders. They had stopped speaking long ago.

The passage had circled and turned back on itself many times. They crawled and rested, crawled and rested, in a nightmarish pattern that repeated itself over and over again. Twice they had fallen asleep and woken in the darkness, crying out to each other in panic. Now they did not know how long they had been in the tunnel. They did not know whether it was day or night. All they knew was that they were climbing. Upward, always upward.

Seven hearts the journey make. / Seven ways the hearts will break. Sheba's words spun round in Rowan's exhausted brain. The Mountain had struck five times. In five different ways five brave hearts had been forced to retreat in shame from their quest: Ellis, Bronden, Val, Allun, Marlie. All gone. Now only he and Jonn remained. The last two hearts for the Mountain to break.

The tunnel narrowed, and he reached yet another turning. With despair he heard the scraping of Strong Jonn's boots and clothes against the rock, the struggling gasps as Jonn heaved himself forward and then lay still. Jonn's every move was hampered by the tunnel walls that gripped him. In all this time he had not been able to reach his flask, or Rowan's, to drink. He was nearing exhaustion. And so was Rowan. If they should come upon a blockage—a fallen rock, anything—they were doomed. Rowan knew that he would not have the strength to move it. And Jonn was tightly wedged behind him. Panic rose in him, as it had so many times since this terrible journey began. He screwed up his eyes more tightly and breathed deeply. He had discovered that this helped.

Star helped, too. Rowan crawled on around the

bend, thinking of Star, the most peaceful and loving thing he knew. He imagined himself walking beside her to the bukshah pool in the evening, his hand on her mane, the cool breeze blowing in his face. The fear died in him. The picture in his mind grew stronger. Now he could almost see the bukshah pool and Star bending her head to drink. He could almost smell the trodden grass, the blossom from the orchard. And he could almost feel the cool breeze on his face. He smiled in the darkness. It was extraordinary. He really could feel that breeze. Just as if—

Rowan's eyes flew open. He stared, licked his lips, and shouted as the cool breeze, the cold breeze, the icy-cold breeze, blew full in his face.

"Jonn," he screamed, "come on! We are there! We are there!" He pulled himself along, faster and faster, careless of his bleeding hands and aching legs, toward the source of that icy wind and the glimmer of white that beckoned him. And behind him, with a last, desperate effort, crawled Jonn.

Agonizing minutes later they were lying together on the floor of a shallow cave that opened to the air. It was freezing. Outside, there was howling wind and the whiteness of moonlit snow.

"Water," croaked Strong Jonn through cracked lips.

Holding the flask to Jonn's mouth, Rowan looked down at him in fright. Jonn's clothing had been torn away by the rock in many places, and the skin beneath was grazed and bleeding. His face was gray. His eyes were closed. The water bubbled from his mouth and dripped to the ground. He shivered without stopping.

Some sticks and dried leaves were heaped in the corner of the cave, blown in by the wind. Rowan gathered them together, found Jonn's tinderbox, and managed to light a fire. It smoked and spluttered, but at least it gave out a little warmth.

Strong Jonn lay still. Rowan waited, his hands clasped anxiously. After a time a little color began to creep back into the man's face. He stirred and opened his eyes.

"We are above the cloud, Rowan," he muttered. "I believe we have been underground for a night and a day and part of yet another night. By this time, if they are safe, Allun and Marlie will be back in Rin. And we are nearly at our journey's end. The map . . ."

Rowan unrolled the map. He followed with his fingers the path they had taken, traced the way above the cloud. "We are almost at the top of the Mountain," he said slowly. "And close to us, very close, there must be another cave or something like

it. Very large. Very deep. The red line ends there."
He swallowed. His eyes had moved to the second-
last blank space.

"And the verse?" Jonn's voice was very weak.
"Read the verse."

Rowan read it aloud, the map shaking in his
trembling hands.

> "Fire, water, earth, and air
> All meet in the Dragon's lair.
> Six brave hearts have failed the test;
> One continues in the quest.
> Remember well the words you know
> When on to find your fate you go."

"So," said Jonn, and closed his eyes again.
Bravest heart will carry on . . .

"But, Jonn, the verse does not speak truly!" cried
Rowan. "There are two of us. Two!"

Jonn moistened his lips with his tongue. "No,
Rowan. I am finished. You must leave me here and
at dawn go on alone. As Sheba foretold." He turned
his head away.

When sleep is death, and hope is gone.

The fire gave a final flicker and went out.

Sleep is death . . .

"Jonn!" Rowan screamed in terror. He shook
Jonn's shoulder savagely, so that the big man stirred

and groaned. "Jonn, do not go to sleep! It is too cold. You are too weak! You will freeze! You will die! Jonn, get up!" Jonn did not move. Rowan sobbed, beating at the ground. "Jonn, I cannot go on alone! You know I cannot! Sheba did not foretell this! Sheba said the bravest heart would carry on. That is what she said. And I am not the bravest heart. I fear everything! Everything!"

Jonn's pale lips curved. "Yes, skinny rabbit. So you do," he murmured. "Fearing, you climbed the Mountain. Fearing, you faced its dangers. And fearing, you went on. That is real bravery, Rowan. Only fools do not fear. Sheba knew that. Sheba knew everything, all along."

Rowan stared. And slowly an icy calm settled on him. He knew what he must do. "Sleep now," he whispered. "I will look after you."

Rowan crept to the entrance of the cave. He took off his jacket and wrapped it around his hands. Then he plunged them into the snow and began to build a wall of snow up around the entrance, filling the gaping space till only a small hole was left for the wind to penetrate. It took a long time, and despite the jacket, his hands were throbbing with cold when at last he was satisfied.

Strong Jonn lay curled up by the ashes of the fire. It was already warmer in the cave but still not warm enough for safety. Rowan pulled on his jacket. Staggering now with weariness, he collected some stones and put them in the ashes, then laid over them the two torches he and Jonn had carried through the Mountain. He lit the torches and watched them flare up, then settle down to burn slowly. He lay down beside Jonn, cuddling close and warming him with his body.

The torches would heat the air. They would heat the stones. The stones would hold the heat after the fire had died. *And hope is gone.* . . . No, the verse had reckoned without him. He still had heart, and hope. Now, with luck, the dawn would find both him and Jonn alive. Then they would see.

Rowan closed his eyes at last and slept.

His sleep was deep and dreamless, and when he woke, he thought at first that no time had passed. But then he saw the pale light that streamed into the cave through the hole in the snow wall and became aware of the silence. It was dawn, and the wind had dropped.

Rowan sat up and with beating heart peered at Jonn. He was warm—and breathing.

Gently Rowan shook his shoulder. "Jonn," he whispered. "Jonn! Wake up. It is morning. And we must go. Together."

*   *   *

They pushed their way through the snow, Strong Jonn leaning on Rowan's shoulder. Their boots sank into the soft whiteness as they walked, squeaking and crunching it into holes that shone icy blue. The tracks of animals that had hunted for food in the night crisscrossed their path, but the animals themselves were not to be seen. Once Rowan thought he saw a sharp nose twitching in a burrow, but in the blink of an eye, whatever it was had disappeared.

Thick cloud floated around them. Above them it cleared to a light haze, and through it they could see the sky. It was a clear, pale pink. A fine day in Rin, thought Rowan, glancing behind him, though he knew he would see nothing. Rin was somewhere there below, but the cloud hid it from view. He felt Jonn's compass in his pocket, the map in his belt. With these, I will find the way back, he promised himself. However long it takes, I will bring Strong Jonn back to Rin. I will see Mother again, and Star, and the bukshah pool in the dawn. I will!

He faced ahead and squinted into the cloud, trying to see. Jonn was struggling beside him, his breath coming hard and fast. Now he was leaning more heavily on Rowan's shoulder, but still, he moved on without complaint. Rowan was filled with pity for his suffering and wonder at his courage.

"All well, Jonn?" he asked as cheerfully as he could. "Nearly there now." And he was struck by a sudden memory. An echo of Strong Jonn's voice, saying those very words to him in just the same way, on that first morning, as they walked away from Rin. Rowan caught his breath. Had Jonn's heart been aching for him then as his ached for Jonn now? And for the same reasons? Had he then been wrong, quite wrong, about Jonn all along?

"Rowan!" Jonn clutched his shoulder. "I think I see something."

A shape rose within the cloud, behind a natural wall of snow-covered rocks. It was white on the edges and pale, shining blue in the middle. It was huge, high, and wide. Above it there was only sky.

"We are at the top," breathed Rowan. His heart began to race. "But—"

Slowly they moved closer. And as they did so, they understood. The whole tip of the Mountain was hollow, making a vast cavern of rock, snow, and ice. The cavern's walls soared to the heavens, flashing in the rising sun like white fire. *Fire, water, earth, and air* . . . A thick carpet of powdery snow covered the ground from its entrance to the wall of rock where they stood.

Rowan stared. There was no sound. No tracks marked that flat carpet of snow. Nothing at all had crossed this place for a day at least. Perhaps many days.

He helped Jonn over the rocks, and they walked to the cavern entrance and cautiously peered inside. White. Nothing but blinding white and shadowy blue. Huge icicles fringed the entrance and the roof. Weird ice shapes covered the walls, rose from the floor. And everywhere there was snow. Their eyes were dazzled. They moved forward, blinking, climbing over the ridges and drifts that covered the floor, gazing in wonder.

Rowan turned to Jonn to speak. Saw his face change. The look of horror—

And then the ground erupted beneath their feet. Snow scattered, and a mighty tail lashed, hurling Rowan onto his back, throwing Strong Jonn crashing to the wall. And Rowan, screaming, watched as the back of the cave came to life, opened its blood-red eyes, and lunged for him, shaking snow and ice from its shining white scales, baring its dripping teeth. Huge. Ancient. Terrible. The Dragon of the Mountain.

13 ∽ THE ANSWER

Rowan screamed, waiting for the hot breath, the tearing fangs and claws that would mean death. But they did not come. He uncovered his eyes fearfully. The Dragon was very near. It was watching him. Its flat, snakelike eyes stared into his, compelling him.

"Jonn," called Rowan in a low voice, without looking away. "Strong Jonn?"

"I am here," came the answer. "The creature's tail has me pinned to the wall. I cannot move. Rowan, save yourself if you can."

The Dragon growled. It turned its head toward Jonn's voice, then looked back to Rowan. It swayed its huge body and clawed at the soft place in its neck, where dried blood crusted wounds made over many days. Its eyes were red pools of anger and—

something else. Rowan saw it and in amazement recognized it for what it was: dumb animal pain.

He slowly got to his feet, never breaking his gaze. "What ails you?" he said quietly, in the voice he used for the bukshah.

The Dragon lowered its head and opened its jaws. It moaned, deep in its throat. Needle-sharp teeth dripped watery blood on the snow at Rowan's feet. Hot, stinking breath beat in his face. Rowan shrank back, but again the Dragon did not strike.

"Rowan!" hissed Strong Jonn. "Back away slowly and go. You have the map and the compass. You can get home. You have a chance. Take it!"

Rowan barely heard him. He was looking at the claw marks around the Dragon's neck. An idea forming in his mind suddenly became crystal clear. He glanced around the cave. No bones or flesh. Just fresh white snow.

"You have not been eating," he crooned to the Dragon, as if he were talking to Star. "You have not been hunting. Yet your jaws drip blood." He met the Dragon's eyes. Long ago, in a very different place and in a pair of very different eyes, he had seen that look before. If he could earn the beast's trust . . . He made his decision and took a deep breath. "I think I know what is wrong. And I can help you," he said. "I am a friend. A friend."

The Dragon stared at him, unblinking.

"Be still," said Rowan.

He moved closer. He looked into the red and dripping mouth, then leaned inside, farther and farther, till he found what he sought.

Look in the fiery jaws of fear, / And see the answer white and clear.

The bone was sharp and white. It had jammed between a tooth and the back of the Dragon's throat, as a twig had once caught in Star's throat. Rowan had removed that twig. He could remove this bone.

He worked gently, knowing the agony the creature was feeling. The Dragon growled. One wrong move, and those terrible jaws would snap closed. Little by little Rowan eased the bone loose. At last, with a delicate twist, he pulled it free. He backed out of the Dragon's mouth and toward Strong Jonn, holding the bone in his hand.

"Now," he said softly. "Now let us go. You are well. You can hunt. Let us—"

The Dragon's eyes flashed. It rose up on its hind legs. It beat its scaly white wings. At last it was free of the terrible pain that had stilled its roar and quenched its fire for so many days. The pain that had stopped it from hunting, wheeling through the skies above its cloudy kingdom. It was free—and hungry.

It roared, and the sound was like thunder, beating and echoing around the walls of the lair. Icicles fell from the cave roof, smashing and splintering on the ground, and the ground itself shook. It roared again, and sheets of fire belched from its mouth and nostrils, melting the snow and ice so that steam billowed into the air to mix with flame and choking smoke.

Then it turned to Jonn. Hunger burned in its red eyes. It would not yet attack the boy who had healed it with his gentle hands. But the man was a different story.

"No!" shouted Rowan. He ran to Jonn's side, slipping and sliding on the now-icy floor of the lair. He threw himself down by the helpless man and shielded him with his body.

The Dragon twisted and roared, and Jonn cried out in agony as the movement crushed him even more firmly against the cavern wall. Rowan pulled out his knife and stabbed desperately at the Dragon's tail, but the knife blade bent and broke against the shiny white scales. It was useless. The Dragon howled with rage and spat a wall of flame that singed Rowan's hair and eyebrows. Again and again the roaring flame came at them. They huddled together.

"Rowan," groaned Jonn. "Rowan, it is trying to scare you off. It only wants me now. Get out while you can, for Jiller's sake, if not for your own. Rowan, I promised her. I beg of you. Go!"

But Rowan would not give in. He had to make the Dragon move its tail so that Jonn would be free to run. He had to do it before the Dragon lost patience and killed them both. But he had no weapons. "What will I do?" he cried out. "I don't know what to do!"

Remember well the words you know . . .

"What words? What words?" Rowan whimpered. "Oh, please . . ."

"The map." Strong Jonn's voice was faint beside him. "Rowan . . ."

Crouching low, Rowan pulled the map from his belt and unrolled it.

Remember well the words you know.

The last blank space was filled. The words swam before his eyes. The words he knew indeed. The words that he had heard for the first time with a thrill of dread, the words that had filled his dreams and haunted his thoughts in the long days since:

Seven hearts the journey make.
Seven ways the hearts will break.
Bravest heart will carry on

When sleep is death, and hope is gone.
Look in the fiery jaws of fear
And see the answer white and clear,
Then throw away all thoughts of home,
For only then your quest is done.

All the prophecies had come to pass, except the last. The last, and the most terrible. And now it was time.

Rowan rolled up the map and drew Jonn's compass from his pocket. He waited his moment.

Throw away all thoughts of home . . .

The Dragon threw back its head and again roared its anger. Its soft neck, scratched and torn by its own claws in its efforts to dislodge the choking bone and end the pain, gleamed pale and exposed.

And with all the strength and desperation of his fear, Rowan hurled the compass at that white, tender target. It struck, like a hard, sharp stone, and the Dragon cried and thrashed in pain and fury, tossing its head from side to side, lifting its tail from Strong Jonn's body.

Just for a moment. Just long enough for Rowan to pull Jonn free, to drag him, sliding, over the icy ground, toward the entrance of the lair. Just long enough for him to turn and throw the rolled map hard, straight and spinning, to strike the exposed neck again, so that again the Dragon roared and for precious seconds turned its head away from them.

Throw away all thoughts of home . . .

Then they were running. Running from the lair. To find a place to hide, to burrow like the night animals, away from the Dragon's rage.

For only then your quest is done. Yes, the quest was done. Done, and lost. As they were. "Mother . . . Star . . ." Rowan sobbed. His heart was breaking. Yet still he ran.

But the snow before the lair had melted in the Dragon's fire, and now the flat surface was a sheet of swimming ice. Rowan and Jonn slipped and fell, their hands flailing helplessly, their feet sliding from beneath them as they struggled to rise and run again.

The Dragon's red eyes burned. It raised itself in anger. Sheets of fire, hot as a hundred furnaces, burst from its mouth and nose, scorching their feet, boiling the ice to a hissing mass of water and steam. Rowan and Jonn rolled, crawled, beating at the melting ice, twisting their bodies to save themselves.

Then, with a screeching crack, the ice split beneath them, the ice that had formed and lain unmelted all the long days of the Dragon's pain, but now at last was feeling the heat of its flames and giving way. The cold, sweet water from the melted snow poured through the ice and into the underground channel that was its old escape from the mountaintop. And with it fell Jonn and Rowan, gasping and shocked, tossed like corks in the bubbling rush. Rowan drew breath, struggled to regain his feet. They were beneath the earth. Beneath the ice. He could no longer see the Dragon. He could no longer see the sky. The water was pushing him. He could not resist it.

All was darkness and glassy-smooth rock, freezing water and rushing sound. Rowan called for Jonn and grabbed for his hand. All at once, he knew what had happened. They had found out the secret of the stream. Sweet water foamed around them, pushing them along. They had released it from its icy prison. Now it was free to flow. And flow it would, down through the long, steep tunnel that was its track through the Mountain's core. And it was taking them with it. Down, down, to the village of Rin.

Val and Ellis had been woken before daybreak by a feeble tapping on the mill-house door. They had opened it to find a nightmare: Allun and Marlie, filthy and ragged, nearly fainting from exhaustion and thirst. They had taken them into the mill, bathed their wounds, and given them food and drink. Then they had heard something of the fearful journey the two had shared as they retraced their steps through the swamp and forest to the clifftop and down to the Mountain's foot. They exchanged grave looks as they learned what had happened in the caves.

"Strong Jonn was a brave man," Val said at last.

"You speak as though he were dead!" Allun cried, pushing his cup away.

"If he is not," Val replied stolidly, "he soon will be. And Rin with him. He is on the Mountain, alone. He cannot succeed now. And he cannot survive."

"He is not alone," Marlie objected. "Rowan is with him."

Val and Ellis stared at her as though she were mad.

"Of what use to Jonn is a scared weakling like Rowan?" Val demanded. "He needs a strong, courageous companion to—"

"He had five strong, courageous companions." Allun lifted his head and looked her straight in the eye. "They all ran away."

Marlie buried her face in her hands.

Ellis finally spoke. "Dawn is breaking. We must go to Jiller," he muttered. "She will be in the buk-shah fields, seeing to the beasts. We must tell her what has happened."

With heavy hearts the four left the mill. The sky was golden pink by the time they reached the dried-up pool. They saw Jiller standing there with

Annad, her shawl pulled tightly around her head. She was looking up at the Mountain, shivering in the cool wind. Then she turned and saw them. The sadness on her face became terror. She screamed. "Allun! Marlie! What has happened? Where is Rowan? Where is Rowan?"

At that moment the roaring from the mountain-top began. And it went on, and on, and on.

Star raised her head and called to Annad and Jiller. Annad did not hear. She had her arms around Dawn's new calf, comforting it as it trembled at the sound of the Dragon. And Jiller, deep shadows under her red-rimmed eyes, was standing rigidly between Allun and Marlie. She heard nothing but the thundering sound high above them on the Mountain, saw nothing but the flashing fire that lit the sky above the cloud.

Val and Ellis stood silently by. With them were Bronden and every other member of the village. All had come running when they heard the sound. Now they stood, looking up, their faces masks of dread and fear. None of them paid attention to Star's call.

Star moved away from the empty drinking pool and began to walk upstream, along the dry streambed. She did not know why she was drawn this way. She only knew that she must go. And quickly.

A fence blocked her way. She nudged it aside with her shoulder, trampled over it without a glance, and moved on.

She heard Jiller's shout behind her, and other voices, but she did not look back. The silent call was stronger now. She broke into a lumbering run.

"Star! What is it?" They were chasing her. She could hear Jiller's sobbing voice and the sounds of many feet. She ran faster.

The streambed gaped brown and empty beside her. Earth, grass, and flowers scattered beneath her hooves.

The mill was ahead, on the other side. The tall stone mill, with its huge wooden wheel that had stood silent for so many days.

And yet . . . Star's ears pricked. There was a sound. A creaking sound. And a rippling, rushing sound. Water! Her parched throat ached for water. But there was another sound, too. A voice. A voice she knew.

"Star! Star! Star!"

Star answered the call. She plunged into the dry streambed. She thundered to the place where the sound came from, the mill channel up ahead, where the great wheel creaked and strained. Sweet water! Her nostrils were full of the smell of it now. For the water was coming, in a wave that rose higher and higher every second, tumbling between the banks of the stream, pushing at the mill wheel's wooden paddles, pouring through it and past it, down to Rin.

Star met and breasted the wave head-on. She tossed her head and heaved herself through the foam, ignoring the sticks and rocks that beat against her legs, ignoring the urge to stop and fill her parched mouth. She forced her way across the earth bank to the mill channel that lay beside the stream. And with a groan of love, relief, and pleasure, she reached the mill wheel and thrust her muzzle into the reaching hand of the boy who clung there.

She dipped her head to take the burden he guided onto her broad back and felt clutching hands on her mane. Slowly and carefully she waded into the foaming stream and through it to the opposite bank, not looking back as the great wheel finally gave way to the pressure of the water and began to turn, crushing the branches and sticks caught between its blades. She clambered from the water. She felt Rowan's hands gripping her wool as he stumbled beside her. Heard Rowan's voice in her ear.

He was talking to her, as he had always done.

And he was talking to the man lying on her back, telling them both: "It is all right. We are safe. . . . We are home. . . ."

Rowan threaded his fingers more tightly through Star's soft, damp coat. "Home," he said again, tasting the word on his tongue. His mind whirled. Everything had happened so quickly. Their journey from Rin to the Dragon's lair had taken long days and nights. Their return, that terrifying downward slide through the underground stream, had taken minutes.

It seemed unbelievable that he was here, safe in the valley, with the grass beneath his feet and the morning breeze in his face. He screwed his eyes shut, suddenly afraid that this was a dream, and that he was still on the mountaintop with the fire, the ice, the terror and despair. But when he opened them again, the green fields of Rin were still there, and Star, and the stream bubbling beside him. It was true. They were home. They were safe. The water had come back to Rin. And they had come with it.

"Rowan! Rowan!" A cry shrilled in the distance. Rowan looked up. A figure was running toward them, along the stream bank. It was Jiller, calling to him, her arms spread wide. Annad ran a little behind her, and far behind them both surged a crowd. It seemed as if the whole village was there, racing toward him. As the people drew closer, Rowan could hear that they were cheering, shouting, laughing with joy. But his eyes were swimming, and he could not see their faces clearly. He could see only Jiller's as she reached him at last, swept him into her arms, and hugged him as though she would never let him go.

Rowan clung to her, listening to the words she crooned to him over and over again, feeling her overwhelming relief and thankfulness for the return of the child she thought she had lost, and her love, which at last he understood. And in that moment the old, cold ache in his heart melted away like snow before the fire, leaving no trace behind.

Together they lifted Jonn from Star's back and knelt beside him. "I think his leg is broken," said Rowan in a low voice. "He is in pain. But he is alive."

Jonn's eyes opened, and he looked up at the two worried faces bending over him. So unalike, yet so alike. He tried to say something, struggled to rise, then fell back with a groan.

"Jonn, lie still," begged Jiller. "Do not try to speak. There is no need."

The injured man wet his cracked lips with his tongue. "There is a need," he said. Rowan could see that every word was an effort for him, but he was determined to continue. "There is something I must tell you, Jiller. I promised—I promised that I would bring your son home to you. But it is Rowan who has brought *me* home. He made me go on when I would gladly have fallen and died. He fought cold and fire for me when he could have saved himself. He faced the Dragon alone."

Rowan crouched on the grass, one hand in Jiller's, the other resting on Jonn's chest. He had not heard the crowd gathering behind him. He did not see the looks of wonder on their faces as they listened to Jonn's words. But Jonn saw. With a great effort he raised his voice.

"It is thanks to Rowan that the stream flows again," he said. "He never gave up. He would not give up. The smallest and weakest among us proved the strongest and bravest in the end. Rin owes him a great debt."

There was silence. A tiny bird chirped in a nearby tree. And then a tremendous sound rose up. Rowan spun around, startled. He saw cheering people all around him. There were Allun and Marlie, their faces still streaked with mud, shouting and laughing and pounding each other on the back. There was Bronden, clapping her hands, and the millers, Val and Ellis, staring at each other in amazement. There was Neel the potter, his mouth stretched into a vast grin, the people from the gardens, and Timon, the teacher. And all the others. "Rowan! Rowan!" they were chanting. "Rowan of the Bukshah! Rowan of Rin!"

Jonn smiled. "Skinny rabbit," he whispered, and, well satisfied, saw Rowan begin to laugh.

Star rumbled to herself. Quietly she moved away and lumbered to the edge of the stream, filled now to the brim with clear, sweet running water. She listened. Low, joyful bellows from the village reached her ears. The water had reached the bukshah pool.

The herd was safe. Rowan was safe. The stream ran again.

All was as it should be. Star lowered her head at last, to drink.